REST IN FLEECE

A Knitorious Murder Mystery

REAGAN DAVIS

COPYRIGHT

ISBN: 978-1-990228-00-1 (ebook)

ISBN: 978-1-7772359-9-4 (print)

FOREWORD

Dear Reader,

Despite several layers of editing and proofreading, occasionally a typo or grammar mistake is so stubborn that it manages to thwart my editing efforts and camouflage itself amongst the words in the book.

If you encounter one of these obstinate typos or errors in this book, please let me know by contacting me at Hello@ReaganDavis.com.

Hopefully, together we can exterminate the annoying pests.

Thank you!

Reagan Davis

CONTENTS

CHAPTER 1

Saturday, June 12th

Shanice Bickerson rules her domain with awe-inspiring efficiency and a blind, three-legged Jack Russell Terrier named Kilian. She has an important job. As head librarian at the Harmony Lake Public Library, Mrs. Bickerson is a pillar of our community and one strand of the fibre that weaves our tight-knit community together.

The Harmony Lake Public Library is a hub of our small town When residents visit the library, they get more than books. Mrs. Bickerson fosters a haven of community, companionship, and offers programs for residents of all ages.

"I'll be right with you, Megan," Mrs. Bickerson says, smiling and holding up her index finger.

"No worries," I reply.

But she doesn't hear me. Mrs. Bickerson's attention

is focussed on her husband, Boris Bickerson. They're standing at the periodical shelves. Mr. Bickerson crosses his arms in front of his broad chest and furrows his brow. His bushy mustache twitches when he speaks. Mrs. Bickerson's hands are on her hips, and she's shaking her head at whatever Mr. Bickerson is saying. The Bickersons are bickering.

Leaning against the counter, I pretend to browse the display of community flyers while discreetly monitoring the Bickersons in my peripheral vision.

Mr. Bickerson uncrosses his arms and gesticulates animatedly. Mrs. Bickerson throws up her hands in frustration and walks away while he's mid-sentence. Mr. Bickerson stomps his foot, scoffs, and marches out of the building.

"Sorry about that, Megan," Mrs. Bickerson says with a warm smile. Despite their domestic drama, Mrs. Bickerson remains poised. "How can I help you?" She pats her short, black, curly hair, then corrects her posture and squares her shoulders.

"I have a couple of blankets for you," I respond, smiling and placing a bag on the counter. "I have three today and should have more next week."

Mrs. Bickerson peeks inside the bag. "Wonderful!" she exclaims. "Thank you so much for doing this. The more isolated residents in our community love getting these lap blankets."

"Don't thank me," I insist. "All I do is crochet the squares together. It's The Charity Knitting Guild members who knit the squares and organize everything. I'm just their delivery service."

The Charity Knitting Guild teamed up with the Harmony Lake Public Library for their current project: lap blankets for the Outreach Reading Program. Every week, Mrs. Bickerson gathers books and magazines from the library and visits residents who can't get to the library as often as they'd like. This month, she's giving them a lap blanket with their book of choice.

The charity knitters knit the squares and drop them off at my yarn store, Knitorious. I use some yarn and a crochet hook to crochet the squares together into lap blankets, then drop them off at the library.

"It's wonderful having Hannah here, by the way," Mrs. Bickerson informs me as she stashes the bag of blankets somewhere under the counter. "I'm so happy she's working at the library this summer."

"She's happy to be here," I respond. "Thank you for letting me borrow her until the end of the month." It feels and sounds odd to thank someone for lending me my daughter.

Hannah is almost twenty. She just finished her second year of university in Toronto and is home for the summer. She has a summer job at the library, but Mrs. Bickerson let me borrow her until the end of the month while my two part-time employees sip their way through the vineyards of Italy and France on a wine crawl.

Mrs. Bickerson giggles. "It's the least I can do." She

gestures somewhere below the counter. "These blankets mean more than you know to the people who receive them."

Mr. Bickerson stomps back into the library, glances at Mrs. Bickerson, then sneers at Kilian who is resting on a dog bed near the door. Mr. Bickerson huffs, turns, and stomps out again.

I lean over the counter and lower my voice. "Is Mr. Bickerson OK?"

Mrs. Bickerson rolls her eyes and flicks her wrist dismissively. "He's angry about the money I spent on Mysti," she explains. "But she's worth every penny. I get more value from the time I spend with Mysti than Boris gets from the time he spends fishing and listening to stock market podcasts."

"Mysti?" I ask.

"You know," she replies, "the fortune teller who set up a booth at the lakefront?"

"I've seen her around, but I haven't met her," I say.

The town is abuzz about the mysterious fortune teller who arrived here last week. Some people say she's blessed with a gift, and some say she's a con artist whose only gift is separating the residents of Harmony Lake from their money.

"Oh, Megan, you must pay her a visit!"

"Fortune telling isn't my thing..." I start.

"Mysti's gift goes way beyond telling fortunes," Mrs. Bickerson interrupts, her eyes wide with enthusiasm and her voice hopeful. She leans into me. "Mysti can contact the dead," she adds in a whisper.

"Really?" I ask, skeptical and concerned at the same time.

"My parents send messages through her," she whispers, then gives me an exaggerated nod.

Mrs. Bickerson's parents passed away last year, a few months apart, after living long, happy lives. The Bickersons were their caregivers, and the double loss was hard for Mrs. Bickerson. Their deaths left Mrs. Bickerson with an empty nest. The Bickerson children are adults and out in the world, living their lives. Following her parents' deaths, Mrs. Bickerson transferred her maternal fussing to the library. The town benefits, but I'm not sure Mrs. Bickerson does.

"I'm glad you find comfort in your visits to Mysti." I smile, sympathetic to her situation.

My mother died when I was twenty-one. She died shortly after Hannah was born, when I needed a mother more than ever. Almost twenty years later, I still have moments when I would give anything to see her, hear her voice, or ask her for advice.

I hope Mysti isn't exploiting Mrs. Bickerson's grief for money. But if Mrs. Bickerson finds comfort from the "messages" Mysti gives her, maybe it isn't a waste of money.

"Well," I say, pushing myself off the counter and pulling myself up to my full height, "I should get back.

Hannah is alone at the store. I hope you and Mr. Bickerson work things out."

"There's nothing to work out," Mrs. Bickerson says, resolute. "Mysti's gift is priceless. You cannot put a price on the peace of mind she provides."

On my way out, I stop to visit Kilian. When I put my hand in front of his nose, he wags his tail and looks in my direction with his closed eyes, sniffing the air. I tell him he's a good boy, give him a few head rubs and a scratch between the ears.

Today is one of the first summer-like days of the year. The sun is bright, the air is hot, and a warm breeze blows off the lake. I lower my sunglasses from my head to my face and stroll down Water Street toward Knitorious. The sidewalk is busy with smiling people soaking up the sun and window shopping. On the other side of the street, walkers, joggers, dogs, kids, and strollers dot the lakefront park.

I'm wearing my first sundress of the season. Sundresses are one of my many guilty pleasures. Despite living where it's winter up to six months of the year, I have an extensive sundress collection. Today's selection is an-off-the-shoulder maxi dress with purple and blue flowers.

I'm a few stores away from Knitorious when its door opens.

"Megastar! There you are!" April calls, her impossibly long legs skipping toward me. "Hannah said you went to the library." She hooks her arm through mine.

April likes to come up with nicknames that sound like puns of my actual name.

"I did," I confirm. "And now I'm going back to work."

"Not yet." April grins, veering us off the sidewalk and onto the curb. She looks both ways then drags me, running, across Water street.

"Where are we going?" I ask.

"To find out the future," April replies. "There's a fortune teller reading tarot cards in the park. I thought it would be a laugh!"

I love April. She was my first friend in Harmony Lake. We've been best friends since our daughters were in diapers. We met at a mummy-and-me playgroup when I moved here. Our daughters are best friends too. They attend the same university.

"I have to get back to the store," I protest. "Hannah's been alone for a while…"

"The store is empty," April argues. "Hannah said it's been dead all day. She gave me her blessing to kidnap you for as long as I want."

April takes long strides, and I trot to keep up with her. April is tall, and I am short. We're kindred spirits, but physical opposites. She's blonde, I'm brunette. Her hair is straight, mine is curly. Her eyes are blue, mine are hazel. April has a perpetual tan, and I look anemic. I'm not anemic, I just look that way. April's tall, lean body looks like it just stepped off a runway at a Milan fashion show, while I'm shorter and curvy with round hips, big boobs, and a small waist.

"I'm not wearing any SPF," I declare, worried about my exposed shoulders.

"You'll be fine," April assures me. "She's reading tarot cards under a tree. We'll be in the shade."

"I don't believe in fortune tellers and psychics," I protest.

April shrugs. "It's for fun. It's just entertainment. We won't make major life decisions based on what she tells us."

"Do you believe in supernatural stuff?" I ask.

She shrugs again. "I don't know. I mean, I'm open minded. If that makes sense. On one hand, I like to think there's a plan, and all this"—she gestures around us—"isn't just random chaos. But I also like to think we control our own destinies."

This conversation is too deep for a Saturday morning.

The fortune teller is under a huge sugar maple tree. She has a large blanket laid out with a crystal ball, tarot cards, and crystals placed around the perimeter in a circle. A handwritten sign leans against the tree.

MYSTI CALLY ~ SPIRITUAL HEALER ~ GUIDE ~
SOOTHSAYER

"Is that Mr. Bickerson?" April asks, lifting her sunglasses and squinting to confirm her sighting.

"Looks like it," I reply. "I saw him at the library earlier, and he was wearing the same outfit. And his moustache is twitching like when he was bickering with Mrs. Bickerson."

"I'd never guess he's into predicting the future and having his tarot cards read," April observes.

"He's not," I confirm.

I tell her about the heated exchange between Mr. and Mrs. Bickerson, and Mrs. Bickerson's confession that they argued about how much money Mrs. Bickerson spends on Mysti.

We keep a respectable distance and watch their interaction from the shade of a nearby oak tree. They seem oblivious to us, and their discussion appears to escalate into a disagreement. The longer they talk, the more exaggerated their facial expressions become, and their body language grows increasingly defensive. Both parties have their arms crossed in front of them and only uncross them to point or gesture at the other person.

Mr. Bickerson takes an aggressive step toward Mysti and enters her personal space. She seems intimidated and backs up. He steps forward again.

"Is everything OK here?" April shouts, taking long strides to bridge the gap between the shade of our oak tree and the shade of their sugar maple.

I hustle to catch up to her, like a toddler chasing their mother.

"I was just telling this charlatan that the residents of

this town don't appreciate her and her con-artist trickery setting up shop here," Mr. Bickerson booms.

"I think she got the message," I say, smiling.

"I doubt it," Mr. Bickerson says, then looks at April and me. "I'd advise you ladies to keep an eye on your wallets." He takes a deep breath and lets it out. "Have a pleasant afternoon."

April and I say goodbye to Mr. Bickerson's back as he storms away.

"Are you OK?" April asks Mysti.

"I'm fine." Mysti's trembling hands say otherwise. "Some people don't like the messages they receive." She shrugs. "But I can't control what the spirits tell me. I'm just the messenger."

We sit on Mysti's blanket, inside the crystal circle, and decide April will go first. While Mysti shuffles her deck of tarot cards and recites some kind of incantation under her breath, I take in our surroundings. A woman on a nearby bench is reading a book. Her gorgeous sundress catches my attention. It's flowy and a beautiful vivid yellow. The wide brim of her straw sunhat hides her face. She's also wearing sunglasses. I can't distinguish her features. Her nails are the same shade of yellow as her dress. Admiring her dress, I realize the sundress isn't the only thing catching my interest. She's wearing a wide-brimmed sunhat and sunglasses *in the shade*. And she hasn't turned the page of her book the entire time I've been watching. It's odd. It's almost like she's trying to go unnoticed, but she's trying so hard, it's backfiring and making her stand out.

"Earth to Megatron," April says, bringing me back to the here and now. "It's your turn. Mysti wants you to shuffle the deck."

"Right," I say, picking up the oversized cards. "Sorry, my mind wandered."

The cards are too large for my hands, but I attempt to shuffle them before handing them back to Mysti.

"It's not really about the shuffling," Mysti explains, taking the cards and giving them a proper shuffle. "It's more about you having contact with the cards so they can absorb your energy." She smiles.

Mysti is pretty. She has long, light brown, wavy hair and small freckles spray the bridge of her nose. Her brown eyes and smile are warm. Unlike Mr. Bickerson, I don't pick up a dishonest or predatory vibe. She seems timid and vulnerable to me. The word *lonely* comes to mind. I'd guess she's in her late twenties, but her high-pitched, child-like voice makes her sound younger and adds to her air of vulnerability.

Mysti lays out three cards: The Page of Cups, The Tower, and Death.

At first glance, my future doesn't look very optimistic.

"The page is a young man," Mysti interprets, pointing to the first card. "Pages are messengers. This young man will bring you a message."

"A good message or a bad message?" April asks, fully immersed in the experience.

Mysti points to the tower card next to the page of cups and makes eye contact with me. "A message that will turn your world upside down and shake you to your foundation."

"Sounds ominous," I respond.

"Not necessarily," Mysti says. "Sometimes good news rocks our world too. And sometimes something that seems negative at first turns out to be a blessing in disguise."

So much wisdom from one so young.

"What about the death card?" I ask, nodding toward it.

"The death card rarely signifies a literal death," she explains with a chortle. "The death card usually portends a transition from one state to another. Something ends so something new can begin."

"But it can signify an actual death, right?" April clarifies.

"It can," Mysti replies, then looks at me. "But you have to consider the cards around it. A young man will give you a message that will turn your world upside down, and things will never be the same. I can't say if the change will be good or bad."

"When can I expect this young man to bring me this message?" I ask.

Mysti shrugs. "Sooner than you think."

CHAPTER 2

"It was vague. It could mean anything," I say to April in response to her enthusiasm about a mysterious young man showing up any second with a life-changing message. "This is how they operate. My fortune could apply to anyone. About anything. It's a setup, so the next time I talk to any young man, and he tells me anything, I'll believe Mysti's prediction came true and rush back to her with more money."

"She seemed sincere, Megnolia," April insists, opening the door to Knitorious and gesturing for me to go ahead of her. "I'm not saying it's true, I'm suggesting we keep our minds open to the possibility."

"Hey, Hannah Banana," I say to my daughter who's standing behind the counter. I scan the floor around my feet, expecting to find a dog clamouring for my attention. "Where's Sophie?"

Sophie is my corgi. She comes to work with me.

"Eric picked her up. They went to the dog park," Hannah replies. "He said to tell you they won't be long."

Eric Sloane is my boyfriend, dog walker, and the chief of our local police department.

"Was it busy?" I ask, stashing my purse under the counter.

"Other than Aunt April and Eric, only one person came in."

"Do you want to take your lunch?" I ask.

Hannah shakes her head and raises her eyebrows like she knows a secret.

When she shakes her head, her long curls bounce and sway around her shoulders. Hannah has my hair, except her curls are tighter. She also has my eye shape, but her green eyes are a blend of my hazel eyes and her dad's blue eyes. Lucky for her, Hannah inherited some height from her dad, so she's a couple of inches taller than me. We have the same fair skin, and similar hourglass figures. She can thank both of us for her sarcastic sense of humour. I like to take credit for her resourcefulness and intelligence.

"Someone is waiting to see Eric," Hannah says. "He got here a few minutes ago."

April pokes my rib. "A mysterious man," she whispers. "The Page of Cups."

I give the empty store a cursory glance. "Where is he?"

"He's in the back." Hannah jerks her head toward

the backroom. "I thought the fewer people who see him the better."

"Why?" I ask.

"You'll see," she replies.

"Did you text Eric?" I ask.

"Not yet. I wanted to wait for you."

April sighs. "I should get back to the bakery."

April and her wife, Tamara, own Artsy Tartsy, the local bakery. Tamara is a talented pastry chef, and her creations are locally famous. They spoil me with treats.

"I should talk to the mystery man." April and I hug. "Thanks for the glimpse into our futures."

"Aunt April," Hannah blurts out. "You should go with Mum."

Now I'm equal parts concerned and curious. What the heck is going on?

"Do you have time?" I ask April.

"I do now," April replies, her curiosity piqued.

"Maybe Mysti's prediction is coming true," April whispers when we're almost at the door that separates the store from the backroom and kitchenette.

"Doubtful," I whisper in response.

A young man wearing a baseball cap sits at the table in the kitchenette. His head is lowered, and he's focussed on his cell phone. Because of his brimmed cap, I can't make out his face.

"Hi there," I say.

The young man's head jolts up from his phone. Our eyes meet. I hitch my breath to stop a gasp from escaping me and reach out, clutching April's forearm to steady myself. Blinking, I do a double take, stunned by the young man sitting in front of me.

"Holy smokes," April mutters under her breath, "they're identical."

I acknowledge her remark with a barely discernible nod.

"Hi. I'm Jaxon Squires." The young man stands up and takes off his green baseball cap. "You can call me Jax."

Even their voices sound hauntingly similar.

Speechless, I reach out by instinct and shake his extended hand. When he smiles, my knees feel like they might give out. Jaxon Squires is the spitting image of Eric. The resemblance is undeniable. He has Eric's brown hair and eyes, complete with honey-coloured flecks, and Eric's smile. This is what Eric would have looked like twenty years ago. They're even the same height and have the same muscular build. *What's going on? Who is this boy?*

"Megan," I mumble, pulling my hand back. April touches my back reassuringly. I clear my throat. "I'm Megan Martel." I introduce myself in a clearer voice, and plaster a smile on my face. "What can I do for you, Jax?"

"The lady at the library said I might find Eric Sloane here," Jax replies with a nervous chuckle. He rubs the back of his neck the same way Eric does when he's nervous or embarrassed. "I went to the police station, but they said he's not working today. I didn't want to leave a message, so I tried the library." He shrugs. "I thought they might have a town directory or something with Eric's address. The librarian said I should try here."

I pull out a chair and sit at the small table, gesturing for Jax to join me. April joins us, too, sitting in the chair beside me. At a loss for words, I can't stop staring at this Eric-identical young man.

"Is Eric expecting you?" April asks, taking the conversational reins while I compose myself and recover from the shock.

"I doubt it," Jax replies. "We've never met." He wipes his palms on his denim-covered thighs and does his nervous chuckle again. "In fact, I'm pretty sure he doesn't know I exist."

"Why are you looking for him?" I ask, afraid I already know the answer.

"Eric Sloane is my father."

I inhale deeply and hold it. Jax's phone dings, and he looks at it. His facial muscles tense as he reads the screen.

"Is everything OK, Jax?" April asks.

Thank goodness she's here to be my voice when I can't speak.

"Yeah. Kind of," he replies. "A friend of mine is having an issue." He scans the room and nods toward the back door. "Can I use that door? I just want to call my friend to make sure everything's OK." He stands up.

"Of course," I say. "I'll text Eric while you're gone."

"So, I came to the right place?" Jax's eyes brighten with enthusiasm. "Awesome. Thank you. I'll be right back." He smiles.

"Eric has a son?" April hisses when the back door shuts with a thud.

"He's never mentioned it," I respond. "April, if Eric has a son, I don't think he knows."

"The resemblance is incredible. They could be…"

"Father and son?" I ask, finishing her sentence.

"I was going to say twins," she says. "But there's your page of cups and your tower."

She's right. This mysterious young man brought me a life-changing message.

I unlock my phone and text Eric.

Me: There's someone at Knitorious to see you.

Eric: Who?

Me: Jaxon Squires.

Eric: I don't know him. Work or personal?

Me: He says he's your son.

Eric: On my way.

The dog park is a ten-minute walk from here. If they run, they'll be here in five.

I place my phone on the table and take a deep, cleansing breath. *Heavy shoulders, long arms*, I remind myself, then take another deep breath. Heavy shoulders, long arms is a mantra I learned at a yoga class in my twenties. It helps release the tension in my neck and shoulders when I'm stressed.

"Are you OK, Megnificent?" April cups my cold, trembling hand in her warm, steady hand.

"A bit shaky and nauseous," I reply. "And curious. I have so many questions."

"Not as many as Eric, I bet."

April gets me a glass of water while I peek my head into the store to make sure it's not busy and Hannah can cope on her own. She's talking to a couple of knitters who are knitting in the cozy sitting area. I close the door to the store and make sure it clicks. It's difficult enough to keep anything private in this town, without having our family dramas unfold at the store during business hours.

We sit in silence, and I sip my water.

"It's been a few minutes since Jax left," April observes. "Should I check on him?"

I nod, unsure if I hope he's there or hope he had second thoughts and left.

"He's there," April confirms, closing the back door quietly. "It sounds like he's finishing his call."

I nod, both relieved and disappointed.

"Maybe we should take Jax upstairs." She gestures to the stairs that lead to the upstairs apartment. "They'll have more privacy up there."

I open my mouth to agree with April when the backdoor and store door open simultaneously.

Both men enter the room at the same time. They lock

eyes and freeze, stunned by the future and past versions of themselves. An eerie Twilight Zone tension fills the room.

Silence.

Oblivious to the thick fog of tension blanketing the room, Sophie trots in and breaks the silence by lapping water from her bowl, the metal tag on her collar clanging against the metal rim of the bowl. Water drips from her chin when, tail wagging, she prances over to greet me.

"Hey, Soph," I whisper, stooping down to pet her.

"You must be Jaxon." Eric speaks first.

Jax nods. "Eric?"

Eric nods and steps forward. Jax steps forward too, and they shake hands.

"Maybe you and Jax should talk upstairs," I suggest quietly to Eric.

"Good idea," April adds. "I'll take Sophie and help Hannah in the store."

"Don't you have to get back to the bakery?" I ask.

"Nope," April assures me as she walks past me to the door. "No way. Not until after." She opens the door and whistles for Sophie. They disappear into the store, closing the door behind them.

She means after I give her an update. I don't blame her. If our roles were reversed, I wouldn't leave, either.

I touch Eric's arm. He looks at me, and I take the leash and dog toy he's holding.

"If you need me, I'll be in the store." I place the leash and toy on the counter.

"Do you mind if Megan comes with us?" Eric asks, looking at Jax. "She's my partner, and I'd like her to be there."

"Sure." Jax shrugs. A micro-expression of comprehension flashes across his face, and his eyes brighten. "Wait!" He points to me and smiles. "You're my stepmum? I've never had a stepmum before."

"I've never been a stepmum before," I respond, trying but failing to match his enthusiasm.

"Does that mean the girl in the store is my sister?" he asks.

"No," I reply, shaking my head. "Hannah's father and I are divorced."

"Oh, right," Jax responds.

Eric gestures for me to go ahead of him. The three of us climb the stairs in silence except for the fourth step, which creaks when each of us steps on it.

CHAPTER 3

WHILE ERIC INVITES Jax to have a seat, I open the fridge and offer him a drink. There aren't many options because we don't eat or drink here anymore. Before he moved in with me, this was Eric's apartment. The apartment is still furnished, but his personal belongings are gone. The space feels soulless now, like a collection of furniture instead of a home. We should find a new tenant. Now isn't the time to think about that. Focus, Megan.

Jax says yes to a diet soda. I take two cans from the fridge, one for him and one for me.

"Thank you," Jax says when I hand him the can.

The leather chair creaks when he leans forward to place the can on the coffee table. The leather sofa wheezes as I sink into it beside Eric. He shifts closer to me until our arms and thighs touch. His body is tense and rigid, like he's ready for something to happen. He reaches into a nearby drawer and pulls out a small note-book and pen. One of his cop notebooks. He finds a blank page, clicks the top of the pen with his thumb and positions the pen, poised to write.

"Who's your mother, Jax?" Eric asks, using his cop voice. "First name, maiden name, and date of birth."

"Jax isn't a witness you're interrogating," I remind him just above a whisper. "He's a young man looking for his biological family."

"Right." Eric clicks the pen again, and closes his notebook, leaving them on the arm of the sofa.

"It's cool that you're a cop," Jax says. "I want to be a firefighter. I took a firefighting and fire systems program. I just graduated, and I have a few interviews lined up with fire departments in nearby towns."

"Near Harmony Lake, or nearby where you live?" I ask.

"Near Harmony Lake," Jax replies, "so we can get to know each other."

I nod. "You just graduated from college?" Jax nods. "Congratulations. So, that would make you... twenty-one, twenty-two?" I probe.

"I turned twenty-two last month," he replies.

Eric's gaze shifts to the distance, and I can tell he's doing mental math. If Jax is twenty-two, and Eric is thirty-nine, Jax was conceived when Eric was.... SIXTEEN!? Oh my. I sip my diet soda and swallow hard. Beside me, Eric's body and posture relax. He lets out a sigh of either relief or disappointment. I hand him my can of diet soda, and he takes a sip, then hands it back to me.

I sit in silence, sipping my soda while Eric and Jax talk. Jax is from Nova Scotia, a province on Canada's east coast. His maternal grandparents, however, are from a small town on Prince Edward Island, another province on the east coast. His maternal grandparents live in the same small town Eric is from. Jax tells Eric his mother's name and a bit about his childhood.

His parents live in Nova Scotia. His mum and stepdad raised him. He grew up believing his stepfather was his biological father. He has two younger sisters.

"When did your parents tell you about your biological father?" Eric asks.

"They didn't," Jax replies. "We visited my grandparents when I was eighteen, and someone in their town called me Eric. They said I was the spitting image of you and asked me if I was a Sloane," he explains. "Everything made sense. We never visited my grandparents, they always visited us. I'm sure my parents didn't want anyone to see me and figure it out. The only reason we went when I was eighteen was because my grandpa had a heart attack. Also, I look nothing like my dad or my sisters. And there are no photos of my parents together before I was a few months old. I found you on the internet, and now that I see you in the flesh, I know you're my father."

"Your parents know you're here, right?" Eric asks.

Jax shakes his head. "They think I found a summer

job planting trees in Quebec." He must see the worried expressions on our faces because he quickly adds, "I didn't tell them because I don't want them to feel bad. I had a great childhood. I love my dad, and I don't want him to think I looked for you because I was unhappy, or he was a terrible father."

"I need to speak to your mother," Eric says.

Jax nods. "Should I phone her?"

"If you don't mind," Eric points down the hall. "You can go into the bedroom and speak to her in private."

Jax stands up and takes a deep breath. He taps his phone screen, puts the phone to his ear, and walks down the hall. We listen for the bedroom door to close.

"Babe, he's not mine!" Eric blurts out as soon as the door shuts. "I've been dying to tell you since Jax told us his age and his mum's name, but I think it's best if she explains it to him." He lets out a sigh, rubbing his temples with his thumb and forefinger. His shoulders slump.

Is he disappointed? Is Eric sad Jax isn't his son? Eric always insisted he never wanted kids. But maybe, faced with the possibility of being a father, he's having second thoughts.

"Umm… you looked at him, right?" I ask, worried Eric is in denial. "He looks like you went for a swim in the fountain of youth."

"That means nothing." Eric waves away my statement. "We all look the same."

"We, who?" I ask.

"Me and my brothers," he replies. "We're practically identical. People confuse us all the time."

It never occurred to me that Jax could be Eric's nephew and not his son. Eric is the middle of three brothers. And he's right, they all look very similar.

"Do you know Jax's mum?" I ask.

Eric nods, swallowing the last of my diet soda. "Her parents live down the street from my parents." He puts the empty can on the coffee table. "Jason and Jax's mum were in the same year at school. They had a fling the summer after they graduated."

My turn to do some mental math. Eric's older brother, Jason, is a year older than Eric. If Jax turned twenty-two last month—and assuming he was born after a full-term pregnancy—he would have been conceived in August of the year Jason finished high school. The timing works.

"I swear, babe, I was never intimate with Jax's mother," Eric says as if he can read my mind. "I was a gawky sixteen-year-old, I wasn't intimate with anyone. Jax is Jason's son. To be honest, his existence isn't a huge surprise. Him showing up here, thinking I'm his father, is the surprise."

"Really?" I ask, recalling Eric's surprised expression when he saw Jax for the first time.

Eric nods. "Jax's mum went away to university. Soon after she left, there were rumours she was pregnant. Jason contacted her and asked her if she was pregnant and if it was his. She denied it. The rumours died down. Then we heard rumours she had a baby. Jason told our parents about their fling, and our parents knocked on her parents' door. They insisted the baby wasn't Jason's. They said she met someone at university, and it was his. But we always wondered."

"Wow," I respond, rubbing his slumped shoulder.

I'm about to ask him how he feels about Jax not being his son, when the bedroom door opens.

"Eric." Jax appears in the doorway, holding out his cell phone. "My mum wants to talk to you."

Eric squeezes my knee and stands up with a sigh. He takes Jax's phone and disappears into the bedroom, closing the door.

The leather chair moans when Jax drops himself into it. He picks up his can of soda and takes a swig.

"I guess you're not my stepmum, after all," Jax says after swallowing the soda.

"No, but I'm excited to have a new nephew," I say, trying to reassure him.

"I feel like such an idiot." He shakes his head. "I was so sure Eric was my father."

"You were close," I console him. "Did your mum tell you who your father is?"

Jax nods. "Jason."

"How are your parents?" I ask. "They must be shocked."

"My dad's not home. He's driving my sister somewhere," Jax explains. "My mum is shocked. The three of us are going to talk tonight. She's not mad though."

"I'm sure all of you will get through this," I assure him. "Jax, where are you staying in Harmony Lake?"

He finishes his soda and crushes the can with one hand. "A place near the highway called the Hav-a-Nap motel. Have you heard of it?"

I nod. "I have. Nice place. But we have a spare room…"

Jax smiles and shakes his head. "That's nice of you, Megan, but I'm staying with a friend as a kind of favour. I don't want to go back on my word."

"I get it," I respond. "I'll give you my number. If you want a hot meal or anything, call me." I hold out my hand and wait for Jax to hand me his phone so I can put in my information.

"Eric has my phone," he reminds me, pointing toward the bedroom.

I reach for the notebook and pen Eric left on the arm of the sofa and write my number on a blank page. I tear out the page and hand it to Jax.

"Your mum wants a quick word before she hangs up," Eric says, entering the living room and thrusting the phone toward Jax.

"How did it go?" I ask Eric when Jax closes the bedroom door.

"I have to call Jason and tell him about Jax," Eric replies. "I'm not looking forward to it."

"I'm sorry," I say, unsure if I'm sorry Eric has to be the bearer of shocking news, or if I'm sorry he doesn't have a son.

He puts his hands on my waist and pulls me toward him, kissing my forehead. "Thank you for your support. I love you."

When Jax returns, I excuse myself to check on the store and leave them alone to talk.

"ARE YOU A STEPPARENT?" April asks when I walk into the store.

"I'm an aunt," I reply.

I tell her about the revelation that all Sloanes look alike, and Jax is Eric's nephew, not his son.

"Eric must be relieved," April comments.

"I think so?" I say, uncertain.

"You *think* so? What does that mean?"

"I don't know," I admit. "Eric was either relieved or disappointed. I couldn't tell. He kind of... deflated when he realized Jax was his nephew."

"I'm sure it was a relief," April says. "Eric is happily child-free. He's been adamant about not having kids. He wants to focus on his career."

"I know," I agree, "but I sense regret." I shake my head and pull myself out of my thoughts. "Where's Hannah?"

"I sent her home," April replies. "I hope that's OK. It was dead in here, and she missed her lunch. Also, she's excited about her date with Lucas tonight, so I told her to go home and get ready."

Lucas Butler is Hannah's boyfriend. He's a rookie cop with the Harmony Lake Police Department.

"It's fine," I say. "I would've done the same thing."

April pulls out a bag from under the counter.

"One of the charity knitters dropped this off." She places the bag on the counter. "She said you'll know what to do with it."

I open the bag. More knitted squares for lap blankets. Without counting, I'd say there's enough here for two blankets.

"Thank you for watching the store, and for taking care of me when I was in shock. You're a good friend."

She hugs me tight. "You'd do the same for me, Megawatt."

"Tell T I'm sorry I commandeered you for the afternoon."

T is what we call April's wife, Tamara.

"It's fine. Both kids are working at the bakery today anyway, so it's not like she was short-staffed."

April and Tamara have two kids, Rachel, who is Hannah's best friend, and Zach, a sixteen-year-old hockey player with a mammoth-sized appetite.

April leaves, and a little while later, Jax leaves too. He pops into the store to say goodbye on his way out.

The store isn't busy, but it's steady. Two customers ask me about the rumour that a young version of Eric is roaming around town, looking for Eric. I'm not surprised. This is a small-town hazard. Everyone knows everyone else's business, and secrets are almost impossible to keep.

I don't confirm or deny anything. Instead, I feign ignorance and say, "Hmmm. That's interesting. Let me know if you find out anything."

CHAPTER 4

Sunday, June 13th

"Wow," Adam says, whisking the hollandaise sauce. "I can't imagine not knowing Hannah existed until she was twenty-two years old. This must be hard for Jason."

"I know, right?" I agree, sautéing the fiddleheads.

Fiddleheads are a local spring vegetable. They're a cross between asparagus, okra, and green beans. They often grow in the wild and are only available for a few short weeks each year.

Adam is my ex-husband and Hannah's dad. When we split up, we started a tradition of having Sunday breakfast together. It was a way for us to spend family time with Hannah while she was at university, but we continue the tradition when she's home for summers and holidays too. When she's at school, Hannah joins us by video call, and when she's home, she joins us in person. We alternate between my house and Adam's condo, but he always cooks. Adam learned to cook when he moved out, and I'm thrilled to let him do it after I did all the cooking during our twenty-year marriage.

"Morning, Dad," Hannah says, kissing Adam's cheek.

"Good morning, Princess," Adam says. "You didn't have to dress up for us," he teases.

She's not dressed up, just less casual than her usual Sunday morning attire of jammies and a messy bun.

"I'm not dressed up, and it's not for you," Hannah justifies. "Lucas is picking me up later. I'm going with him to look at apartments." She smiles.

Adam does not smile. He pinches his thick, dark brows together and narrows his blue eyes. He's beating the hollandaise sauce so hard you'd think it insulted his mother.

This is Hannah's first adult relationship. Adam is struggling with not being the only man in her life.

To distract from her father's reaction, I ask Hannah to set the table. When she leaves the kitchen, I take the fiddleheads off the stove and whisper to Adam, "Your disapproval is showing. Maybe you can tuck it in."

He grunts in acknowledgement.

I ignore Adam's reaction, intent on not arguing with him.

"Ready?" I ask cheerily in my normal tone of voice.

"Ready," Hannah and Adam say in unison.

33

As we settle in for a yummy breakfast of eggs benedict and sauteed fiddleheads, Hannah asks me where Sophie is.

"Eric took her to the dog park," I reply. "Again. It seems to be their new favourite place."

Hannah smirks and pushes her fiddleheads around her plate.

"How does Eric feel about his new nephew?" Adam asks.

I shrug. "I think he's still processing it. He hasn't said much since he talked to his brother yesterday."

Adam and I are still close. When our marriage ended, we were determined to keep our family intact and be friends. We still love each other, but not the romantic way spouses should. We forged a new friendship based on our shared past and mutual love for our daughter. Despite this, I don't share with him my suspicion that Eric is disappointed Jax isn't his son.

"I'll call Eric later. See if he wants to go golfing to take his mind off it," Adam suggests between mouthfuls.

"Good idea," I agree.

Yes, my ex-husband and boyfriend are friends. And yes, it's weird sometimes. Eric was new in town and didn't know anyone. Adam didn't have any friends here because he was a workaholic who spent most of his time at his office in the city. He was a senior partner at a large law firm, but since we split up, he left the firm and opened a practice in Harmony Lake. We spend more time together divorced than we did married. Adam is our town's only lawyer, and as of earlier this year, he's also the mayor. He and Eric bonded over a mutual love of golf, and the rest is history. Their friendship is another non-traditional piece of our modern family.

"Lucas and I are going to a bonfire tonight," Hannah adds. Adam rolls his eyes at the mention of Lucas's name, but Hannah doesn't notice because she's focused on cutting her egg. "We can invite Jax to come with us. He can meet some people." She shrugs.

"That's thoughtful, sweetie. Thank you." I smile.

"Did you tell Connie about Jax?" Hannah asks.

Connie is my surrogate mother and Hannah's surrogate grandmother. She took us under her wing when we moved to Harmony Lake. She's the original owner of Knitorious, and now that I own the store, she works for me part-time. Connie is getting wine-drunk in Italy and France with her friends until the end of the month. She sends us daily texts with photos from her European adventures.

I shake my head. "I'm waiting until the DNA results are back," I explain. "You know how Connie is, she'll worry. I don't want to interfere with her trip. She's looked forward to this tour for months."

"Do you think Jax will stay in Harmony Lake now that Eric isn't his father?" Hannah asks.

"I'm not sure," I answer honestly. "He has interviews lined up with local fire departments, but I don't know if this will change his plans."

"Is Jason planning to meet Jax soon?" Adam asks.

"Jason and his wife are flying in sometime this week," I tell them. "They have to make childcare arrangements and book time away from their jobs. Eric said Jason will let us know when they confirm their travel plans."

"Will they stay at chez Martel?" Hannah asks.

Chez Martel is the nickname for our house. Adam is French, so at the time it seemed fitting.

"We think they'll be more comfortable in the apartment above the store," I explain. "They'll have more privacy, and it'll give them somewhere to spend time with Jax."

"Makes sense," Adam comments.

I tell them Eric and I are going to the apartment later today to give it a thorough cleaning and stock the kitchen and washroom with some essentials before Jason and his wife arrive.

"I hope Jax is a real Sloane and doesn't just look like one after all the trouble you're going to," Hannah comments.

"Jason ordered a DNA test," I disclose. "They'll ship one swab to chez Martel and the other to Jason PEI. He ordered it with overnight shipping. Jax's swab should arrive today."

PEI is short for Prince Edward Island, Canada's eastern-most and smallest province.

We finish eating, and Adam and I pour ourselves a second cup of coffee when Hannah's phone chimes.

"Something came up and Lucas is running late," she announces with a slight pout. She puts her phone on the table and takes a deep breath. "Can I ask you something?"

We nod.

"You know how the apartment above Knitorious is just sitting there? Empty?"

"Yes," I reply with a nod.

Under his breath, Adam mutters, "No way," like he knows what she's about to say.

Hannah either doesn't hear him or ignores his comment.

"Would you consider renting it to Lucas?" she pleads. "He's been searching for a decent apartment for months. There's, like, no rental housing in Harmony Lake aside from vacation rentals, and everything else is too far from work. He commutes for, like, an hour. One way." She lays out her argument like a lawyer. She is her father's daughter.

I look at Adam. He looks at me. His jaw is tense, and he's flaring his nostrils. He doesn't like this conversation.

"We'll think about it," I tell her.

"Think about what?" Hannah asks. "You have an empty apartment, and Lucas is a rent-paying tenant. He's a cop, so the store would be safer with him there," she argues. "You and Dad own the apartment, so it's not like you have to ask anyone."

Actually, I own the store and the apartment. I also own the house—now with Eric—and Adam owns his condo and the law practice. I own both cars, and our investments are still joint. It's complicated. Sometimes I find it confusing, so I can see why Hannah is confused. It's difficult to divide assets after a long marriage, so we left most of them commingled for the sake of simplicity.

"Eric's stuff is still in the apartment, Princess," Adam says. "Let us think about it, and we'll talk to you and Lucas about it soon."

"Thank you," Hannah says, standing up. "I'm going to finish getting ready."

"Leave it, sweetie. We'll take care of it," I say when she motions to pick up her plate.

After a quick peck on the cheek for each of us, Hannah disappears, and moments later, her bedroom door closes with a dull bang.

"We're losing her, Meg," Adam says with a heavy sigh.

"We aren't losing her, Adam. She's growing up. She still needs us, she just needs us differently," I say, not sure if I'm trying to convince myself or him.

"Lucas monopolizes her time. And he's too old for her. She's too young to be this serious about a *boy*."

He spits out the word *boy* like it leaves an unpleasant taste in his mouth.

"My dad said the same things about you," I remind him.

"She shouldn't be helping him find an apartment. At her age, she should have fun with her friends and hang out at the lake."

"Hannah and Lucas are the same age you and I were when we got married," I point out.

Hannah will be twenty in August, and Lucas just turned twenty-three; the same ages Adam and I were on our wedding day.

Adam freezes and looks up for a second. I'm sure he's doing the math, intent on proving me wrong.

"It's not the same thing, Meg, and you know it." He sips his coffee.

"I know you aren't happy about Hannah and Lucas's relationship, but she's an adult, and we can't choose her partner," I say. "It would help if you could be supportive."

"I don't like him," Adam insists.

"You don't know him," I counter. "The four of us should have dinner together."

Adam's eyes narrow, and he taps his fingers on the table. "Clever, Meg," he says. "Maybe if you, me, and Eric have dinner with Hannah, we can convince her that Lucas isn't right for her…"

"No," I interject, waving my hands. "That's not what I mean, and you know it. I mean you, me, Hannah, and Lucas should have dinner together. We'll take them to a restaurant. Somewhere neutral. We can get to know him, and he can get to know us."

"Can Eric come?" Adam asks.

"No." I shake my head.

"Why not?"

"You know why not," I reply. "Eric is Lucas's boss and the chief of police."

"Exactly," Adam says.

"You're the mayor, which is intimidating enough. We want Lucas to feel comfortable, not threatened."

"*You* don't want him to feel threatened," Adam mumbles, rolling his eyes.

"Pardon?" I say, pretending I didn't hear him.

"Nothing," he mumbles.

"Try to treat Lucas the way you wish my dad treated you."

"Fine," Adam cedes with a sigh. "We'll have dinner, and I'll keep an open mind."

CHAPTER 5

WE ZIP along the highway between Harmony Lake and Harmony Hills. The day is bright and clear. Eric and I are on our way home to Harmony Lake to drop off some essentials we picked up for the apartment.

Harmony Lake is a tiny town and doesn't have the same amenities as larger towns. We don't have big-box stores, chain restaurants, or a movie theatre, for example.

"How's Jax today?" I ask. "Have you spoken to him?"

"We exchanged a couple of texts. He seems fine," Eric replies. "We're going to meet after dinner to do the DNA swab."

"Why don't you invite him for dinner?" I suggest, looking through the window and admiring the cloudless blue sky against the mountains.

I don't mind making trips back and forth to Harmony

Hills. I'd rather live in my picturesque, cozy town than in the suburbs any day. Harmony Lake is on the south side of the Harmony Hills mountain range. We're sandwiched between the mountains and the lake. There's no room for expansion, but nature gave us the perfect setting for a tourism-based economy. Tourists flock to Harmony Lake in the summer to be near the lake, and they flock to us in the winter to ski, snowboard, and skate.

Right now, we're on the cusp of tourist season; the tourists are just trickling into town. After the July long weekend, throngs of city-escapees will descend on Harmony Lake until Labour day.

"I don't think that's a good idea, babe," Eric replies.

"Why not?"

"Because we don't know him. He's a stranger who literally showed up out of nowhere twenty-four hours ago."

"He's your nephew," I remind him.

"That doesn't mean he's a good person," Eric explains. He places a hand on my knee. "I know you want everyone to feel welcome and included, and I love that about you, but we don't know Jax. I'm uncomfortable with him having that kind of access to you and Hannah. We should get to know him better before we welcome him into our home."

Now would be a bad time to tell him I already offered Jax our guest bedroom and told him to call me if he wants a home-cooked meal.

"OK," I agree, smiling.

"I'll run his name when I get to the office tomorrow, and we'll take it from there."

Eric's phone rings. His car has Bluetooth, so he answers it hands free, and the caller's voice echoes through the car's speaker system.

It's dispatch. There's a dead body at the Hav-a-nap motel.

"That's where Jax is staying," I say. "Oh my god, Eric! What if it's him?"

Eric presses his foot on the gas pedal and asks the dispatcher for more details. The deceased is a woman. There are no obvious signs of foul play.

I blow out a relieved breath.

"Want me to take you home?" Eric asks without taking his eyes off the road.

"No way."

AS WE APPROACH THE MOTEL, uniformed officers detour traffic to prevent rubberneckers from seeing the crime scene. We slow down as they wave Eric through, moving pylons and tape to accommodate his car.

"You know the drill," he reminds me. "Touch nothing. Stay in the car." He gives me a side glance. "Well, do your best to stay in the car."

"Got it." I nod and jerk my thumb toward the backseat where my bag is. "I brought lap-blanket squares. I'll crochet them together while I wait."

Eric complains that I never stay in the car at a crime scene when he asks me to. Is he right? Maybe. In my defense, I only exit the car with good reason. As a compromise, I text him to let him know where I went.

The police cordoned off the parking lot at the Hav-a-nap motel with police tape. Most of the action is at a north-facing room. Officers in white bunny suits enter and leave the room. Bunny suits are not rabbit costumes, they're what the police call the white HAZMAT-type suits that the forensics people wear to minimize contamination when they are at a crime scene.

Eric pulls into an empty spot near the motel office, turns off the engine, but leaves the fob key in the cupholder between us.

"Text me if you need me." He smiles and winks, making the butterflies in my tummy flutter.

I nod.

I turn on the stereo and use my phone to set my playlist to shuffle. As the opening bars of Wonderwall by Oasis fill the car, I twist my upper body and retrieve my bag from the backseat. Through the back window, I glimpse Carlo Viscardis, the manager of the motel. He's sitting alone on the curb smoking a cigarette. For an instant, I debate getting out of the car to check on him. I decide against it because, for once, I'd like to surprise Eric by actually staying in the car.

I open the window to let in some fresh air, then pull

the knitted squares from my bag. I lay them across my lap and begin moving them around, arranging them until I'm satisfied with how they look. With my phone, I snap a picture of the final arrangement, in case they get mixed up later, then I stack them in the order I'll crochet them together.

"Hey, Megan."

I'm rummaging through my bag, searching for my crochet hook, and almost jump out of my skin when I hear my name so close to my ear.

"Hi, Carlo," I say, hand on my chest. He's leaning in the open window with his forearms resting on the door. "You startled me. I didn't hear you coming."

"How could you with the music so loud?" he teases with a grin.

It's not *that* loud.

"You want to get in?" I jerk my head toward the driver's seat next to me. He nods.

Carlo walks around the front of the car and climbs in. I turn off the music and rest my hands on the bag in my lap.

"Lots of excitement today," I say, stating the obvious. "How are you doing?"

Carlo's chest expands when he inhales deeply. "Anxious," he replies. "A housekeeper found her. She was pretty shaken up. The police are talking to her now."

"Did you see the scene?" I ask.

He shakes his head. "I stood guard until the police

arrived but didn't go in. The housekeeper said the dead woman was on the bed, fully clothed. She was face down and her upper body was lying on the bed and her feet were on the floor. Like she fell forward onto the bed, or something." Fidgety, Carlo picks at the fabric of his cotton trousers. When I glance at his hairy knuckles, I notice his hands are trembling.

I sympathize. I tremble around death too.

"It sounds like it wasn't violent," I say, looking for a bright side to this tragic event. "Maybe she had a heart attack or something."

"I'm not a doctor or anything," Carlos disclaims, "but I think she was too young for a heart attack. Unless she had an underlying condition or something," he speculates.

"How old was she?" I ask.

He shrugs. "I dunno, late twenties or early thirties." Beads of perspiration dot his brow. He seems nervous. It's not hot in here. I press the button on the armrest and lower the driver's side window. The cross breeze is refreshing.

"Is she staying in the room alone?" I ask, wondering if her family knows what happened.

"She checked in alone, but a friend joined her a couple of days ago. He wasn't there when the house-keeper found her."

"Well, you have her name and address from when she checked in, right? The police might ask for it to notify her family."

"She paid cash, Megan. I don't know her name or address," he admits, sounding nervous about the transaction. The cross breeze isn't stopping the beads of perspiration from forming on his brow. Now they're forming in the thick stubble on his upper lip too. Carlo is the type of man who has a five o'clock shadow by noon. "She paid for a week in advance. She signed the registration form as M. Cally." He shrugs. "We called her Ms. Cally."

Carlo's twitchy demeanour is making sense. A guest who wanted to remain anonymous died under mysterious circumstances in her room.

I flashback to the handwritten sign leaning against the tree the fortune teller sat under yesterday.

MYSTI CALLY ~ SPIRITUAL HEALER ~ GUIDE ~ SOOTHSAYER

"Wait." I reach out and touch Carlos's arm while I connect the mental dots. "Is the dead woman the fortune teller everyone is talking about?"

Carlo nods. "That's her."

Mysti is dead.

CHAPTER 6

A POLICE OFFICER comes to the car and asks Carlo to go with him.

"My turn to give my statement," Carlo says with a weak smile as he opens the door and gets out.

"Good luck," I say, unsure of the appropriate send-off in this circumstance. "I hope you feel better," I add to cover my bases.

I turn on my music again and find my crochet hook at the bottom of my bag. I sing along to Mysterious Ways by U2, making progress on the lap blanket when the driver's side door opens.

"Wow. I didn't think you'd still be here," Eric jokes with a chuckle.

"Ha-ha," I respond, pleased to have shocked him with my compliance.

"Was it natural causes?" I ask. "Do you know how Mysti died?"

Confusion clouds Eric's face. "How do you know who died?"

"I don't have to leave the car to find stuff out," I tease, not using Carlo's name so he won't get in trouble for talking to me.

"Did you know her?" he inquires. "The fortune teller, I mean."

"I met her," I reply, nodding. "She read tarot cards for me and April yesterday."

"I didn't think you believed in that kind of thing," he comments with a smirk.

"I don't," I confirm. "It was for fun. It was April's idea, and I promised her I would keep an open mind."

"Do you believe in fortune tellers and psychics?" I ask, knowing Eric is a show-me-the-evidence kind of guy.

"No." He chuckles, rubbing the back of his neck with his hand. "But I didn't believe in women's intuition before I met you, and now I trust your intuition more than actual evidence sometimes."

"You say the sweetest things." I lean over and give him a quick kiss.

"Did you have any other interaction with her?" he probes.

I shake my head. "No. She read our cards, then April and I went to Knitorious where Jax was waiting to meet you. Are you questioning me?" I ask. "Is Mysti's death a murder investigation?"

"I'm not sure yet," Eric replies. "I'm waiting for the

coroner to look at her and give his opinion. We'll treat it as a suspicious death until we know otherwise." He produces a small, clear, plastic evidence bag and smoothes it on his lap. "We found this in her room."

I look at the contents. A torn piece of paper with my first name and phone number in my handwriting. The piece of paper I gave to Jax when I told him to call me if he needs anything.

"I gave that to Jax yesterday." I gasp and bring my hand to my mouth. "Is Mysti the friend Jax was staying with?" I ask out loud.

"We found men's belongings in the room," Eric admits. "And both beds look slept in. Jax is staying with a friend?" Eric asks. "I knew he was staying at the motel, but he didn't mention a friend."

I tell Eric what Jax said about staying with a friend.

"He sounded concerned about his friend," I say. "It might be the same friend he talked to on the phone before you showed up."

"Did you overhear the conversation?" Eric asks.

I shake my head. "He stepped outside to make the call. He said his friend had a bad day or something. He wanted to check on them."

"Did he mention a name? Or any identifying information."

I wrack my brain trying to recall the details.

"I don't think so." In front of us, a luxury sedan parks and a middle-aged man gets out of the car. He's wearing golf pants, a golf shirt, and a golf hat with the

Harmony Hills Golf & Country Club logo embroidered on the front. "Coroner," I say, nodding toward him.

Eric looks up and waves. The man comes over and leans in the driver's side window.

"Eric! Great day on the links. Too bad you couldn't join us."

"Well, someone has to work in this town," Eric responds. The two men laugh.

"Hello, Megan." He tips his hat. "Long time no see."

"Hi, Raj," I say, smiling. "Shame your round was cut short."

"What room?" Raj asks.

"107," Eric replies. "I'll meet you there in a minute."

Raj nods, tips his hat at me again, and returns to his car where he retrieves what I assume is coroner stuff from his trunk.

"I have to go," Eric says, then leans over and gives me a kiss. "Do you want a patrol car to take you home, or are you taking the car?"

"I'll take the car," I offer. "I need to drop off the stuff we bought at the apartment."

He kisses me again, tells me to drive safely, and gets out of the car.

I pack up my crochet supplies and toss them onto the backseat. Walking around to the driver's side, I see Jax Squires talking to a uniformed officer at the parking lot entrance. Jax is pointing toward room 107, and the officer shakes his head. My uneducated guess is that Jax wants to get to his room, but the officer won't let him.

I pause and bite the inside of my cheek, debating what to do. I know what I want to do. But it could interfere with the investigation if the coroner and police determine Mysti was murdered. The distressed expression on Jax's face helps me decide.

"Hi, Jax!" I say, approaching him and the officer he's talking to.

"Hi, Megan," Jax replies, shocked to see me. "What are you doing here?"

"Wrong place, wrong time," I reply. "Eric is here. I was just leaving." I look at the officer. "Can Jax join me in the car?" I ask, pointing to Eric's black Dodge Charger parked about fifty feet away.

"You can't go near the room," the officer warns Jax.

Jax nods.

"We won't get any closer than the car," I assure the officer. He smiles. "Thank you." I smile.

"What room are you staying in?" I ask Jax on the short walk to the car.

"107," he replies, holding up his room key.

The Hav-a-nap motel is an older establishment, and it predates keycards and other high-tech conveniences most modern hotels have. The Hav-a-nap has real keys. Upon registering, they issue guests an actual key on an oval metal key chain with their room number etched in white. It's quite charming in a retro way.

We get in the car and close our doors slightly out of sync.

"What's going on? Why can't I go to my room?" Jax asks, watching the commotion surrounding room 107.

"Your room is part of a police investigation," I explain. I pull out my phone and unlock the screen. "I'll just let Eric know you're here."

Me: I'm still here. Jax is in the car with me. He was staying in room 107.

Eric: He can't leave with you. We need to talk to him.

Me: OK.

Eric: Text me when you leave.

Me: OK.

"Is Mysti OK?" Jax asks. "What happened?"

"I don't know the details," I reply truthfully.

Two officers position themselves in front of and behind the car, staring at us inside. Courtesy of Eric, no doubt.

"Why are they here?" Jax asks when he notices the officers.

I shrug one shoulder. "It's their job," I say nonchalantly, as if it would be weird if two police officers *weren't* surrounding the car and watching us.

"Is Mysti OK?" Jax asks again.

"I don't think so," I reply.

Panic seizes Jax's face, and his breathing hastens. "He came back for her, didn't he?"

"Who came back for her?" I ask.

"If something happened to her, it's my fault," Jax blurts out, ignoring my question. He's on the verge of hyperventilating. "She was scared, and I told her I would protect her."

In response to Jax's change of demeanour, the officer in front of us takes a protective step forward. I look at him and shake my head. He acknowledges me with an almost indiscernible upward nod.

"Deep breath, Jax." I place a gentle hand on his arm and inhale an exaggerated breath, hoping he'll follow my lead.

Jax and I make eye contact, and he takes a few deep breaths, redirecting his anxious energy to his leg, which bounces with a chaotic rhythm.

"Start at the beginning," I suggest, trying to guide him. "How long did you know Mysti?"

"We met on Friday," he replies. "When I arrived in Harmony Lake."

"How did you become roommates if you just met?" I probe.

"I came to the motel looking for a room," Jax explains. "They didn't have any. They were booked. I was walking back to my car to leave when I saw Mysti in the parking lot arguing with some guy. It looked intense. I assumed she was fighting with her boyfriend or something. I got in my car and monitored the situation for a few minutes. I didn't want to leave if she was in trouble."

"That was very valiant of you," I tell him. "A very Sloane-like reaction."

Jax grins, and I detect a hint of pride at the comparison.

"The dude's body language got more and more aggressive. Mysti cowered, and I could tell he scared her. That's when I went over. The guy backed off as soon as I approached them."

I'm sure he did. Jax is over six-feet-tall and well-muscled. When motivated, I'm sure he could intimidate most people.

"I swear, Megan, I didn't touch the guy." Jax puts his hands in front of his chest, palms forward. "I stood between him and Mysti and asked him if there was a problem. He said there was no problem. I suggested he was just leaving, and he agreed. He turned and high-tailed it away from us."

"Did you hear any of their argument?" I probe.

Jax shakes his head. "When I approached them, he was jabbing his finger toward Mysti,"—Jax jabs his index finger into the air in front of him—"and he said, *it'll be the last thing you ever do!*"

Sounds like a threat to me.

"Did Mysti tell you his name?" I ask.

"No," Jax replies. "But she made it clear he wasn't her boyfriend. She said she didn't know him. She didn't tell me much. I got the feeling she was afraid."

I got the same feeling yesterday when April interrupted Mysti and Mr. Bickerson's interaction.

I unlock my phone and open a social media app.

"Is this the man who was with Mysti?" I show him a picture of Boris Bickerson.

Jax shakes his head. "No. The dude she was arguing with was younger than him."

"Have you seen him since?"

Jax shakes his head. "No. But I hung around after he left. You know, in case he came back. Mysti asked what room I was in. I told her they were booked, and I couldn't get a room. She offered me the spare bed in her room."

"Just like that?" I ask, bewildered. "She offered her spare bed to a huge guy she just met?" This sounds unbelievable to me.

Jax nods. "I think she was scared," he surmises. "She relaxed a lot when I accepted her offer. I got the feeling she felt safer with a roommate. And that was fine with me. I like to help people."

Another Sloane-like trait.

If what Jax says is true, Mysti must have been beyond scared. I would have to be downright terrified for my life before I'd ask a big, scary stranger I just met to share my motel room.

"You need to tell this to Eric," I tell him.

"Mysti's dead, isn't she?" Jax asks. "Was she murdered?"

"Yes, she's dead," I reply. "But they don't know yet if it was murder. They're gathering evidence, and the coroner is examining her. They'll know more about how she died soon. In the meantime, they have to treat it like a crime scene."

"In that case, there's more I should tell you," Jax says.

"Like what?"

"Mysti was on the run."

"From the police?" I ask.

"From her family."

"Was she escaping an abusive relationship?"

"I don't think so," Jax responds. "It had something to do with a family business. Mysti said her family wanted to kill her because of the family business. She thought they had hired a hit man to take her out. That's why she moved from town to town. She was trying to stay ahead of the hit man. She planned to leave town tonight. Someone owed her money, and they were supposed to pay her today. She said as soon as she got the money, she was outta here."

"Did Mysti think the man you saved her from was the hit man?"

Why would a hit man risk being seen by arguing in public with his target?

Jax shakes his head. "She said he was a dissatisfied customer."

"Why didn't Mysti go to the police if she feared for her life?"

"She thought the police would arrest her because of her scam."

"What scam?" I ask.

"She moved from town to town offering her services as a fortune teller," he explains. "She chose small towns because they have a lot of gossip. When she arrived in a new town, Mysti would change her look and blend in with the locals. She'd hang out at the local gathering places like pubs, parks, libraries, and stuff. She kept her eyes and ears open for gossip and personal stories, learning intimate details about the town's residents and their lives."

"Mysti confessed to you that her gift was fake," I say. It's a statement of fact, not a question.

Jax nods. "After she learned about them, she would set up her fortune-teller booth," he continues. "When the locals came to her for spiritual guidance, she would amaze them with details about their lives and problems. Believing her gift was real, they'd give her more money for more guidance."

Jax says Mysti was skilled at reading people and asking questions. When answering her questions, Mysti's clients unknowingly disclosed private information about their friends and family—also town residents —that Mysti would use in her readings with those people.

I'm processing what Jax is telling me and watching room 107. Eric just exited the room and is heading toward the car, no doubt to talk to Jax.

"Where were you this morning?" I ask.

"I went to a restaurant for breakfast, then hung around the waterfront. I waited for Mysti to come and set up her booth, but she didn't show up. I texted her and phoned her, but she didn't answer. I thought maybe she left town without saying goodbye. I came back to the motel to check on her. Instead, I found you and a crime scene."

After Jax's explanation about Mysti's scam, I feel vindicated that my instincts about her gift being an elaborate swindle were right.

Her gift might have been fake, but it sounds like Mysti Cally the fortune teller may have predicted her own murder.

CHAPTER 7

ME: I'm in the lobby.

Eric: I'll be right there.

The secure door opens, and Eric appears. He holds the door, and I stride through it into the inner workings of the Harmony Lake Police Department.

"This is a nice surprise," he says as we stroll down the corridor. "You hardly ever visit me at work."

"Because I don't want to distract you," I tease with a wink as we enter his office.

"You distract me whether you're here or not," he says quietly, then taps my bottom.

Shocked, I spin around to make sure no one saw, relieved to see he'd closed the office door behind us.

With a glint in his eye, Eric smirks and cocks an eyebrow. "How do you plan to distract me?" he asks as he leans against his desk.

A familiar tingle of temptation tugs at me down low,

but I remind myself why I'm here and banish all inappropriate thoughts from my mind. *Focus, Megan.*

"A courier delivered this to the house about an hour ago." I reach into my bag and hand him the box from Let Me Take A Cellfie; the box that contains Jax's half of the DNA test. "Also, I thought you might want your car back." I hand him his keys.

"I'll get a patrol car to take you home," he says, putting the keys and DNA kit in his desk drawer, then sitting on the sofa adjacent to his desk.

"No need," I tell him. "Hannah's coming to pick me up. She came home to get ready for the bonfire tonight, and I asked her to pick me up in my car."

"Thank you for dropping that stuff off." He pats the sofa cushion next to him, coaxing me to join him.

"There's more," I inform him, ignoring his invitation. "I thought you might be hungry." Eric is always hungry, so this assumption isn't much of a stretch on my part. I sit next to him, put my bag on the floor, and pull out a glass food-storage container. "Chicken wraps and pasta salad for you." I hand him the container and pull out a second, identical container. "And for Jax." I hand him the other container. "I assume Jax is still here?"

"He's still here," Eric confirms, putting the containers on the end table next to the sofa. "His statement was long. He's waiting to sign it before he can leave."

"He had a lot of information considering he only knew Mysti for two days," I concur.

"Do you believe him?" Eric asks, narrowing his eyes and rubbing his thumb and forefinger along his chiseled chin.

"That he only knew Mysti since Friday?" I clarify.

He nods.

I sink back into the sofa and sigh.

"I'm not sure," I admit. "He seems sincere, but I don't know him well enough to know if he's lying. Also, I find it hard to believe that Mysti, a woman travelling alone, would invite a guy she just met to share her motel room. Especially a guy like Jax. He's physically intimidating."

Eric nods in agreement. "I had the same thought."

"Do you suspect Jax and Mysti knew each other before Friday?" I ask.

He shakes his head. "There's no evidence to support that," he says. "Using receipts and social media posts, we traced Jax's trip from Nova Scotia to Ontario. He didn't cross paths with Mysti, and he wasn't in any towns she visited."

"You traced Mysti's whereabouts before she came here?" I ask, amazed.

"It wasn't difficult," he replies. "She left a path of angry people in her wake." He stands up and picks up a file folder from his desk, then sits back down. "She lived as a transient fortune teller for a few months. Mysti Cally wasn't her only alias. She also called herself

Lady Karma, Luna Soleil, and Claire Voyant. She scammed people in small towns, and several of her victims filed police reports."

"People can file a police report because the fortune teller they paid was a fraud?" I ask.

He opens the folder and shows me several grainy and low-quality photos of what *might* be Mysti, but I can't say for sure. Most of them look like still shots taken from surveillance camera footage.

"The scam she told Jax about wasn't Mysti's only scheme," Eric explains. "According to the complaints, Mysti used the more scandalous information she learned about people to blackmail them."

Chances are, not everyone who Mysti blackmailed went to the police. If they filed a complaint, they'd have to tell the police what information Mysti used to black-mail them, a conversation some victims might prefer to avoid. The reports that Eric uncovered likely represent only a fraction of her victims.

"This explains why she told Jax the police would arrest her if she went to them for help," I deduce.

"She's wanted in at least three jurisdictions," Eric confirms.

Anyone Mysti blackmailed or swindled in these towns could have hunted her down, seeking revenge.

"So, if Mysti was murdered, the suspect pool would be huge," I speculate.

"There's no *if*," Eric corrects me. "Mysti Cally was murdered." He opens the folder again and flips through the pages. "The coroner found these." He removes two sheets of paper from the folder and hands them to me. "The killer stuffed them down her throat after she died."

The first sheet is a photo of the death card from Mysti's tarot deck. It has lines and crease marks like someone crumpled it up. The killer must've scrunched it to make it fit in her throat.

"The death card came up when Mysti read my cards," I say.

"How prophetic," he responds dryly.

The next sheet of paper is a photograph of a hand-written note. Like the death card, the note has lines and creases as if someone crumpled it up. The note says: *$10,000 and your secret is safe with me.* It's written in blue ink, on notepaper with the Hav-a-nap motel logo.

Are the death card and the note a message? Or does the killer have a sick and twisted sense of humour?

"I hate to stereotype," I say, "but this looks like a woman's handwriting."

The penmanship is neat and curvy, with rounded letters that are uniform in width and height. The printed letters look like they were written without lifting the pen from the paper. I don't know many men whose penmanship has these characteristics.

"The note was most likely written by a woman," Eric agrees. "I'm waiting to hear from the handwriting expert, but at first glance, she also speculated a woman wrote it."

"Do you think Mysti wrote it?" I ask.

He shrugs. "Possibly. We found samples of Mysti's handwriting with her belongings. The expert will compare them and get back to me. We're testing the pens from the room too. To see if any match the ink on the note."

"Jax said Mysti planned to leave town today. He said someone who owed her money was supposed to pay her today, then she was leaving. Maybe this note refers to the money she was waiting to collect."

"Maybe she blackmailed someone local, and they killed her," Eric theorizes.

"April and I saw Mysti and Mr. Bickerson arguing on Saturday," I say. "We couldn't hear what they were arguing about, but it was intense enough for April to intervene."

I also tell Eric about my conversation with Mrs. Bickerson at the library on Saturday morning, and the Bickerson's domestic dispute near the periodical shelves.

"Did the tarot card and note cause Mysti's death?" I ask. "Did she choke on them?"

Eric shakes his head. "The coroner thinks the killer smothered her with a pillow from the motel room," he confides. "He found a few fibres inside her nose. They're being tested against fibres from the room. He said he'll know more after her autopsy. If she was smothered, he expects to find more fibre samples in her lungs."

The mental images of the autopsy and the smothering make me shudder. Eric puts his arm around my shoulder and pulls me into him.

"Since Mysti Cally was an alias, how will you notify her family without her actual name?" I ask.

"We found her ID in the motel room," Eric explains. "Her driver's license, bank card, and credit cards."

"What's her real name?" I ask.

Eric sits up and rifles through the papers in the file, and hands me a photocopy of Mysti's driver's license. She was twenty-nine years old and had an upscale Toronto address. Her name was Everley Leighton Moregard-Davenhill.

"Wow! Impressive moniker," I comment under my breath.

"She probably got writer's cramp signing her name," Eric jokes. "No wonder she shortened it to Mysti."

"That's not what I mean," I clarify. "The Moregard-Davenhills are one of the wealthiest families in the world."

Eric sits up at attention, pulling himself up to his full seated height.

"You've heard of them?" he asks, incredulous.

"You haven't?" I reply, equally incredulous. "The Moregard-Davenhill family owns MD Biocorp, one of the largest biotech companies in the world. You use their products every day. They make the vitamins and supplements you take and the cold medication we keep in the medicine cabinet." I stand up and open his desk drawer, removing the Let Me Take A Cellfie box. "See?" I hold it in front of him, pointing to the small print that says: Let Me Take A Cellfie: a division of MD Biocorp.

"Wow," Eric declares, shaking his head. "I had no idea."

"Is MD Biocorp the family business Mysti told Jax about?" I wonder out loud.

It feels wrong to call her Everley. She introduced herself as Mysti, and that's the name she called herself, so it's what I'll call her too.

"This changes things," Eric says, sitting at his desk and making notes on a piece of paper in Mysti's file. "I assumed she was talking about a regular family business, not a multi-billion-dollar, multinational corporation."

"Maybe Mysti was right about her family being out to get her," I suggest. "Considering who her family is and the amount of money that could be at stake, maybe she wasn't exaggerating. Maybe when she told Jax she feared for her life, she had a legitimate reason to be scared."

"I need to find out more about her relationship with her family and her role in the business," Eric says. "It's possible she's a distant relative and has nothing to do with the business."

"True," I say. "Have you contacted them yet?"

"I'm waiting for someone to call me back," he

replies. "This isn't the kind of news you leave in a voicemail message."

Fair point.

Deep in thought, our eyes meet, and we're struck by the same idea simultaneously. We both look at the laptop on Eric's desk. He taps on the keyboard, and I rush around to his side of the desk where I can read the screen over his shoulder.

According to the internet, Everley Leighton Moregard-Davenhill was a major shareholder of MD Biocorp, along with her parents and two siblings. All family members own an equal number of shares. It would take three family members to control the company, which sounds like a recipe for a family feud.

"And the list of potential suspects gets bigger," Eric mutters under his breath.

While he prints some of the information we found online, I settle on the sofa and unlock my phone to snoop Everley Leighton Moregard-Davenhill's social media accounts.

She was active on social media, posting almost every day, and sometimes multiple times a day. Her most recent post was... an hour ago?! Impossible! She died over six hours ago. I scroll below the post to read the comments. She responded to a comment less than fifteen minutes ago. This must be a fake account. But it looks so real.

"What's wrong, babe?" Concern seeps onto Eric's

face as he stands up. "You look like you've seen a ghost."

"Sort of," I acknowledge as he joins me on the sofa.

I tilt my phone and show him my post.

"What the?" he mumbles, taking my phone and scrolling down to the comments like I did moments before. "It has to be fake," he insists.

Speechless and confused, we stare at the post in silence. It's a photo of a takeout coffee cup from a national coffee chain with the name Beverley hand-written on the side of the cup in black marker. The caption reads, "When you place the same order at the same coffee shop every day, and they still get your name wrong." Followed by a facepalm emoji.

"We don't even have one of those coffee shops in Harmony Lake," I point out.

"Someone else must have access to Mysti's social media accounts," Eric concludes. "It's the only explanation. Otherwise, this is a very convincing fake account." He opens his phone and types something. "I'll look into it," he says.

Someone knocks on the door.

"Come in," Eric bellows.

"Hi, Jax," I say.

"Hi, Megan," he replies.

"Eric, I signed my statement."

"Good," Eric replies. "Megan brought your DNA swab. Want to do it now?"

"Sure." Jax nods with enthusiasm.

I sit on the sofa and watch while Eric and Jax open the box and read the instructions. Seconds later, Jax swabs the inside of his cheek and drops the swab in a vial. I offer to take the swab with me and drop it off at the post office tomorrow. With any luck, we'll have the results in a couple of days and at least one mystery will be solved.

"Are you hungry?" I ask Jax.

He nods, rubbing his stomach. "I haven't eaten since breakfast."

I shoot Eric a dirty look, and Jax adds, "Eric offered me lunch, but I wasn't hungry. Not after what happened to Mysti."

I give him a sympathetic smile. "How are you feeling now?"

"Hungry."

I hand him one of the glass containers.

"Go find the lunchroom," Eric instructs. "I'll meet you there in a few minutes, and we'll have dinner together."

Jax thanks me for the food and closes the office door behind him when he leaves.

"I can't tell you how many people have commented on the resemblance," Eric says, shaking his head.

He's referring to the resemblance between himself and Jax.

"How do you explain it?" I ask.

Eric shrugs. "I ignore it."

"How's Jax doing?" I ask. "A murder investigation

on top of finding your biological family is a lot to process."

"I think he's over the shock, and he's cooperative with the investigation," Eric replies. "There are no available rooms at the Hav-a-nap. He can't go back to room 107 because it's a crime scene. Is it OK with you if he stays in the apartment above Knitorious tonight?"

"Of course, it's OK with me," I say.

"I'll stay with him," Eric adds. "I don't know him enough to know if he's really OK. And he's a person of interest. I need to make sure he doesn't leave town."

"Has Jax told his parents what's going on?" I ask.

"I suggested he call them, but he refused. He said they'll panic and book plane tickets. He doesn't want to worry them."

"Jax seems like a considerate, caring person," I say. "Very Sloane-like," I add with a smile. "Does Jason know Jax is involved in a murder investigation?"

Eric nods. "I told him. He told me to keep him updated," he says, his voice full of disappointment. "I don't get it, babe. Jason's so casual about Jax. Jason and his wife haven't even firmed up their travel arrangements yet. And he only spoke to Jax on the phone once, for two minutes, and hasn't reached out to him since." Eric shakes his head and leans against his desk, crossing his arms in front of his chest. "I don't understand how he can be so uninterested." He shrugs and shakes his head. "If I had a kid somewhere, I'd drop everything and go there."

"I know you would," I say, running my hands up and down his biceps. "Your brother might need more time. His situation is complicated. Jason has a wife and three kids who are affected by this. Lucky for Jax, he has an attentive uncle in the meantime."

I knew it; I saw it in his eyes when he told me Jax was his nephew and not his son. For a few moments, Eric thought he might be a dad, and the disappointment when he found out he wasn't made him realize he wishes he was.

I've been a parent for twenty years. I love Hannah with all my heart. She's the best thing I've ever done. But I've been raising her since I was twenty-one, and I don't want to do it again. I don't want to go through late night feedings, toddler tantrums, potty training, PTA meetings… just thinking about it overwhelms me.

My phone dings.

"It's Hannah," I say. "She's outside. I should go."

Eric thanks me for dinner and everything else, and we kiss goodbye.

We leave his office together. At the end of the hall, he turns right toward Jax, and I turn left toward the exit.

CHAPTER 8

Monday, June 14th

Early bird that I am, I arrive at the post office five minutes before it opens. Even after taking my time assembling a lap blanket and taking Sophie for a longer walk than usual.

I don't mind waiting outside in the warm morning sun. Most businesses aren't open yet, so Water Street is still quiet. I lean against the wall outside the post office and raise my face toward the sun, listening to the birds in the park across the street.

The ding of my phone distracts me from my meditation.

April: What are you doing out there?

The post office is next door to Artsy Tartsy. April must see me through the window.

Me: Waiting for the post office to open.

April: Are you coming in when you're done?

Me: Of course!

April: I want to hear everything!

Harmony Lake is a small town, and Mysti Cally's death is public knowledge. I don't think her true identity is public knowledge—yet—but her death and the mystery surrounding it is.

Dropping my phone in my bag, I spy someone across the street. They're standing still and watching me, just standing there with their hands at their sides. A woman. Her wide-brimmed, straw sun hat is familiar, but the rest of her isn't. I contemplate crossing the street to talk to her, but the click of the lock on the post office door startles me. I turn and smile at the postal worker as she flips the sign from CLOSED to OPEN. She smiles back and holds the door open for me. I turn to check on the woman across the street. She's gone. Poof. Vanished. Weird.

A few minutes later, I drop off Jax's DNA swab, and I'm on my way next door to see April and indulge in one of Tamara's sweet treats. Leaving the post office, I hold the door for someone struggling to see over the massive box they're carrying.

I step onto the sidewalk and lower my sunglasses to my eyes from the top of my head.

"Excuse me!"

I turn toward the unfamiliar voice.

"Hi," I say to the woman in the wide-brimmed straw sun hat. "Are you talking to me?" I ask.

She nods. "My name is Renée Dukes." She extends

her hand for me to shake, and I immediately recognize her long, manicured, vivid yellow nails.

"Megan Martel," I say, shaking her hand. "I've seen you around."

"I work for the Moregard-Davenhill family," Renée explains. "They hired my firm to locate their daughter."

This must be why Renée was sitting near Mysti's fortune-telling blanket at the park on Saturday, pretending to read the book she was holding.

"How can I help you?" I ask, wondering what Renée could want with me.

"I was hoping we could talk," she replies. "Maybe share some information about Everley's death and her movements before. My client asked me to cooperate with the investigation to the fullest extent possible."

"You should talk to the police," I advise. "I can give you a number for the lead investigator." I reach into my bag and rummage around for my wallet so I can give her one of Eric's business cards.

"Aren't you the police?" Renée asks, looking confused as she takes off her sunglasses.

"No, I'm not." So far, she's not wowing me with her investigative skills.

Renée shakes her head. "I'm sorry. I assumed you were with the police. You were at the crime scene, and yesterday you were at the police station. Also, Everley's roommate was in your car."

How did Renée have such a good view of the crime

scene yesterday? How did she know I went to the police station? Is she watching the police, or Jax?

"You're right," I confirm, "but I'm not with the police." I decline to provide further details about my involvement with the case.

"Well, whatever your involvement, be careful," Renée warns. "I wouldn't invite that roommate into my car if I were you. I think he's the key to what happened to Everley."

It's weird to hear someone refer to Mysti as Everley.

"Why do you say that?" I ask.

"A hunch," she replies, shrugging a shoulder. "I've done this a long time. I have pretty good instincts about people. My instincts about this boy are that he's dangerous. Everley was on the run alone for months and nothing happened to her. Then as soon as this guy shows up, she's dead? That can't be a coincidence."

As much as I hate to admit it, Renée has a point.

From the corner of my eye, I spot April watching our exchange through the bakery window.

"There's a great little bakery right here," I gesture toward Artsy Tartsy. "I was just going to treat myself. Would you like to join me? We can compare notes, and I'll buy you a pastry."

Renée smiles. "Sure. I'd like that. I haven't eaten breakfast yet."

We stop at the counter and assess the yummy, fresh-made pastries under the display glass. We choose one of the secluded bistro tables at the back of the bakery.

Without taking my order, April brings over a medium roast coffee with two sugars and one cream—just the way I like it.

I thank her and she recommends the scones with clotted cream. Renée and I agree it sounds wonderful, and April disappears behind the counter to prepare our order.

"Do you work for the Moregard-Davenhills too?" Renée asks.

"No," I reply. "In fact, I didn't know Mysti was a Moregard-Davenhill until yesterday. Her true identity isn't common knowledge."

"I see," Renée acknowledges. "I suspect we aren't the only firm they hired to find their daughter, but I don't know for sure."

"How long were you looking for Mysti?" I ask.

"Almost three months," Renée replies. "Until Harmony Lake, I've always been one town behind her. She was good at staying hidden. The only reason I caught up with her is because she re-used one of her aliases."

Renée tells me that Mysti hadn't used any credit cards or bank accounts since her disappearance. She left her cell phone at home and has contacted no one from her old life. Whatever Mysti ran away from, she did everything possible to make sure it wouldn't catch up with her.

April delivers Renée's tea and our scones and clotted cream. Then she pulls up a chair from a nearby table and joins us at the small bistro table. Renée looks at me, shocked.

"This is April," I explain. Then I look at April. "April, this is Renée Dukes. She works for Mysti's family."

"Ah," April says with an understanding nod. "It's nice to meet you, Renée."

The two women shake hands, and I explain to Renée that April knows everything I know. Renée seems fine with it.

"When I searched Mysti—erm, Everley's—name on the internet, there was nothing about her being missing," I say, smothering a scone with clotted cream. "In fact, if her social media accounts are anything to go by, she's living her life as usual and joking with friends and family in the comments. "

Renée holds up her finger while she swallows a mouthful of scone. "That's by design," she explains. "Everley is worth *a lot* of money. Her family was concerned for her safety. If her disappearance was public knowledge, and the wrong people found her, Everley would be a target for kidnapping, or worse. The firm I work for hacked into her social media accounts and took them over to create the impression that Everley isn't missing."

This explains how Mysti has continued to post and comment after her death, and why her posts include photos that weren't taken anywhere near Harmony Lake.

"What did Mysti say when you found her?" I ask.

"I never spoke to her," Renée replies, then sips her tea. "I confirmed Mysti Cally and Everley were the same person on Saturday. I notified her family on Saturday evening. They asked me to continue surveillance until they got here. They were making travel plans and said they would be here Sunday night. They didn't want me to approach their daughter and risk her running again. This type of transient lifestyle isn't safe for someone like Everley," Renée continues. "If someone recognized her, she could be in danger. She died the next day, before her family got to Harmony Lake."

"But they knew where she was?" I clarify. "You told them she was staying at the Hav-a-nap and what her alias was?"

"Of course," Renée confirms. "They're my clients, they're paying me to find this information."

So, the night before Mysti's murder, the people she believed wanted to kill her discovered her location. The Moregard-Davenhills might not have come to Harmony Lake themselves, but maybe someone they hired—or even Renée herself—acted on their behalf.

"Mysti didn't know you were following her?" April asks, sounding skeptical.

I'm skeptical too. With her vibrant yellow dress, nails, and giant sunhat, Renée didn't blend in with the crowd. I noticed her on Saturday, and I wasn't even looking for her. Mysti was on the run and afraid; she must have noticed Renée hovering and lurking, pretending to read a book.

"I don't think so," Renée shrugs, smearing clotted cream onto another scone. "I think she would've taken off and tried to lose me if she knew."

"Mysti said she was on the run from her family because she believed they wanted to kill her," I say, watching Renée's face closely for a reaction. None. Her brown eyes and the rest of her face remain relaxed and unresponsive. "She said it was because of the family business but didn't elaborate."

"The Moregard-Davenhills love Everley," Renée insists. "They're concerned for her well-being. Everley overreacted to a family misunderstanding and ran away."

Renée explains that despite being married for over thirty years, in private, Mysti's parents live separate lives and are married in name only. They keep up the facade because their separation would spook investors and hurt the share price of MD Biocorp. In other words, their net worth would take a hit. According to Renée, Mr. and Mrs. Moregard-Davenhill can't be in the same room without arguing. She says they often drag their three kids into their disagreements. It was one of these disagreements that drove Mysti into hiding. Mr. and Mrs. Moregard-Davenhill disagreed on a major business decision regarding the European division of MD Biocorp. To out-vote the other, each parent solicited their children for support in a race to get the majority of votes. Each of Mysti's siblings supported one parent, leaving Mysti as the deciding factor. Whichever parent she sided with would win. Overwhelmed by the pressure, she ran. Renée speculates Mysti misunderstood her parents' and siblings' aggressive lobbying and felt threatened.

"Everley wasn't like the rest of the family," Renée discloses. "She was sensitive and creative. Her parents and siblings are business-minded and analytical. She didn't understand them, and they didn't understand her."

"Where were you when Mysti died?" I ask.

"If she died Sunday morning, I was at the park," Renée responds, "sitting on a park bench and waiting for Mysti to set up shop for the day."

If Renée is telling the truth, and Jax is telling the truth about his alibi, they must've seen each other.

"Did you see Mysti's roommate at the park?"

Renée shakes her head. "I don't think so. Should I? Was that his alibi?"

"I don't know his alibi," I fib. "I'm not the police."

Renée asks me about my involvement with Mysti and the investigation. I answer her questions and tell her April and I met Mysti for the first time when she read our tarot cards on Saturday.

"I saw you on the bench near Mysti's tree," I tell her. "Your yellow maxi dress is gorgeous. I couldn't keep my eyes off it. And the matching nails are a nice touch." I nod toward Renée's fingertips.

Flattered by the compliment, Renée tells me where she bought the dress and suggests it might still be on sale. She opens her phone and texts me a link to the dress at an online store. We now have each other's contact information and I have a dress to order.

Renée asks more questions, which seems fair since I just interrogated her. I explain that I was at the crime scene because I was in the car with Eric when dispatch called him to the motel. I tell her Jax is a relative we don't know very well, who arrived in town two days before Mysti's murder.

"Don't you think the timing is suspicious?" Renée asks. "He shows up and, just like that, they share a room? And now she's dead?"

I do find it suspicious but don't admit this to Renée because I find her suspicious, too, and I don't trust her.

Renée looks at her watch and tells us she has to go. We thank each other for taking the time to talk, and she thanks April for the scones and tea, then Renée leaves.

"What do you think?" I ask April when we're alone.

She shrugs. "I think the Moregard-Davenhills can afford a better private investigator. Instead of blending in, her wardrobe choices make her stick out like a sore thumb. There's no way Mysti didn't know Renée was tailing her."

I nod. "I thought the same thing," I agree. "But that yellow dress she wore on Saturday was so gorgeous."

"Also, I doubt her clients would be comfortable with her disclosing their personal business. Their family dysfunction and secret separation are secret for a reason."

She's right.

"Do you think Renée killed Mysti?" I ask.

April takes a deep breath and lets it out. "I think she's a good contender, unless Eric can confirm her alibi. Or maybe she looked the other way while someone else killed Mysti. Someone sent by Mysti's family."

"If Hannah were missing, I'd tell everyone who would listen," I speculate. "I'd want the entire world searching for her. I wouldn't cover it up like Mysti's parents."

"We're not super rich," April reminds me. "All that money seems to complicate things."

"You're right," I agree, knowing I can't relate to a mother with billions of dollars and a huge corporation to consider. "Is Mysti's family worried about her safety?" I ponder aloud. "Or are they worried the MD Biocorp share price and their net worth would plummet if the media found out someone who controls twenty percent of the company was missing? If the media looked into Mysti's disappearance, they'd uncover the family dynamics that lead to it. What do you think?"

"I think money is the root of all evil," April replies.

Me too.

CHAPTER 9

Sophie's doing a new thing; no matter which toy I throw, she brings back a different one. It's so random. She's never done this before. Until today, she always brought back the toy I threw.

I turn off the hose, throw Sophie's braided rope toy across the yard, then wind the hose around the hook on the wall.

"Hey, handsome," I say when Eric steps out of the house and onto the back deck. "Why are you home in the middle of a workday?"

I'm home because Knitorious is closed on Mondays. Today is the day I clean the house and run errands. Right now, I'm pulling weeds in the backyard, watering the hanging baskets, and playing fetch with Sophie.

"I miss you." He tips the brim of my sunhat and stoops down to kiss me. "And I need to pick up some clothes for tomorrow. I think I'll stay at the apartment with Jax again tonight."

I nod. "How is he today?"

"He seems OK," Eric replies with a sigh. "He's on his way to Harmony Hills for an interview with the HH fire department."

"So he's staying in Harmony Lake?" I ask. "Even though you aren't his father?"

"I don't think he's decided," Eric says. "But the interview was already scheduled. And if it distracts him from Jason and Mysti, it can't hurt."

"I'm sure you're right," I agree.

Sophie drops her green tennis ball at my feet.

"Watch this," I say, picking up her frisbee and throwing it.

Sophie scampers after it, skidding to a halt when she reaches the frisbee's landing place. But she ignores it. Instead, she sniffs around and finds an orange tennis ball nearby, picks it up and prances back to me proudly, dropping it at my feet.

"Good girl, Soph!" Eric crouches down and rubs the corgi.

"Don't you think it's strange?" I ask, wondering why he didn't comment that she switched toys. "I threw the frisbee, and she brought me the ball," I explain in case he missed her switcheroo. "She's never done this before, but she's been doing it all day."

"Hm." Eric shrugs. "Who knows?"

I guess it's not a big deal. It's just weird.

"Does she do it when you take her to the dog park?"

"Speaking of the dog park," he says, ignoring my question, "I was hoping to take her today, but I don't think I'll have time. Maybe I'll ask Hannah to take her after her shift at the library. What do you think?"

"She'll survive," I say. "I walk her three times a day," I remind him. "Skipping the dog park for one day won't traumatize her."

"I know," he says, "but she has friends there, and Sophie loves the dog park. Besides, it's part of her routine now."

Whatever.

"Lemonade?" I ask, taking off my hat and using the back of my hand to wipe beads of sweat from my brow.

"I brought you an iced vanilla latte," he responds. "It's in the kitchen."

"Just when I think you couldn't be more perfect." I stand on my tippy toes and give him a thank you kiss.

Eric pours himself a glass of lemonade while I wash my hands and freshen Sophie's water.

"How's the case?" I ask, joining him at the kitchen table and sipping my latte.

"More complicated than yesterday," he says with a sigh. "The fingerprint report landed in my inbox this morning." He unlocks his phone and opens the email. "They found four sets of prints that could be of interest."

"OK," I say with a sneaking suspicion he's about to drop a bombshell.

"Jax Squires."

Not the bombshell I was expecting.

"He was staying in the room," I remind him. "It would be more suspicious if Jax's fingerprints *weren't* there."

"Renée Dukes."

"How did you get a fingerprint sample from her?" I ask.

"She's a licensed PI, her prints are on file," Eric explains.

"Renée didn't say anything about being inside Mysti's room," I say, recalling our conversation at Artsy Tartsy this morning. "In fact, Renée told me she never spoke to Mysti."

"You spoke to Renée Dukes?" he asks, wide eyed and incredulous. "She's coming to the station later. I haven't even spoken to her yet."

I nod. "She approached me this morning outside the post office." I shrug a shoulder. "We had scones and clotted cream at Artsy Tartsy with April."

I tell Eric about my conversation with Renée and her theory that Jax murdered Mysti.

"She lied to you," Eric says when I finish my recap. "She didn't contact the Moregard-Davenhills on Saturday night. I spoke with Mysti's parents myself. They haven't heard from Renée in almost a week."

"Maybe the Moregard-Davenhills are lying," I suggest. "Maybe they killed Mysti and don't want to admit they knew where she was."

"Renée is a private investigator. If she killed Mysti, she'd be smart enough not to leave fingerprints behind," Eric surmises.

"I don't know," I rebut. "She wasn't smart enough to figure out I'm not a cop. Or to turn the page on the book she pretended to read."

"Who did the third set of prints belong to?" I ask, redirecting our conversation back to the fingerprint report.

"Boris Bickerson."

This is a small bombshell.

"Oh my." I sigh. "I wonder why he was in Mysti's room."

"Possibly to murder her," Eric states.

I can't tell if he's being sarcastic.

"I mean, assuming Mr. Bickerson didn't kill Mysti," I clarify. "Why would he go to her room? Was he trying to get Mysti to give back the money Mrs. Bickerson paid for readings?"

"I'd ask, but the Bickersons lawyered up," Eric says. "It's not as easy for me to question them now."

I wonder if they'll talk to me? I add The Bickersons to my mental to-do list.

"It's possible the killer didn't leave fingerprints in Mysti's motel room," Eric reminds me. "In fact, if they're smart, they didn't."

Why is he managing my expectations? Is it because the next name is the bombshell I've been expecting?

"Who is it?" I ask, cutting straight to the point.

"The last set of prints belongs to Lucas Butler."

Yup. There's the bombshell. Kaboom!

"Hannah's Lucas?" I ask, wide-eyed and stunned.

Eric nods.

"What did you say about Lucas?" Hannah asks, walking into the kitchen.

"Aren't you working at the library today?" Eric asks, surprised.

"Her shift ended at noon," I tell him.

While Hannah pours herself a glass of lemonade, Eric tells her that the police found Lucas's fingerprints in Mysti's motel room.

"Of course, his prints are there!" Hannah declares, like it's the most obvious thing ever. "It's a crime scene, and he's a cop." She shrugs.

"He didn't work yesterday," Eric reminds her. "Lucas wasn't at the crime scene."

Panic and confusion cloud my daughter's face.

"Don't worry. I'll get to the bottom of it," Eric assures her. "I'll talk to Lucas this afternoon."

"No need," I say with confidence. "I think Lucas is being summoned by a power greater than his boss." I nod toward Hannah who's tapping her phone like a fanatic.

"An angry girlfriend is scarier than I could ever be." Eric smirks and I playfully swat his shoulder.

Hannah either doesn't hear us or ignores us as her thumbs fly across the keyboard. Her phone rings while she's still typing.

"Tell him to stop whatever he's doing and come to the house," Eric says as she accepts the call.

Hannah puts the phone to her ear and disappears into the next room.

"Where were Lucas's prints?" I ask, hoping to come up with a reasonable explanation. "Were they in one specific location?"

Eric shakes his head. "They were all over the room, babe," he discloses. "Every doorknob, light switch, even the shower door."

I sigh. "Were the police ever called to room 107 before Mysti died?" I ask, grasping for reasons to explain why Lucas's fingerprints would be all over Mysti Cally's motel room.

"No," Eric confirms. "I checked."

"Do you think Lucas and Mysti had an affair?" I whisper.

Eric shakes his head. "There's no evidence to support that."

Except his fingerprints all over her room and on her shower door.

"Lucas cares about Hannah. He'd never mess around behind her back," I say, trying to convince myself.

My heart thumps double time. Just thinking about the possibility that Lucas two-timed my daughter makes me flush with anger. I take a long sip of my iced latte to cool off.

"I think Lucas Butler is a stand-up guy," Eric assures

me. "I don't think he'd mess around." He rubs my shoulder. "Also, he knows Adam and I would kill him," he mutters under his breath.

"Don't say that!" I admonish. "This is a murder investigation. It's not funny. Even if you're joking."

"Who's joking?" he asks. "What if Lucas can't explain these fingerprints? Am I supposed to look the other way if he cheated on my stepdaughter?" Now Eric's flushing with angry heat.

Eric and I aren't married, so Hannah isn't his step-daughter. But he's so riled up about Lucas's fingerprints in Mysti's motel room, that I let it go without correcting him.

We talk about marriage often. Because Eric brings it up often. He's made his intentions clear; Eric wants us to get married. I want us to get married, too, but I'm not ready yet. I'm still getting used to living together.

Eric and I met just as my marriage to Adam was ending. I had a post-divorce plan that included being single and living alone—something I'd never done. Meeting a kind, thoughtful, gorgeous, funny man and falling in love was not part of the plan, but here we are. Eric's latest negotiation tactic is a long engagement, which is hard to argue with. So I agreed, provided we don't have to set a date yet. I know he's planning to propose any minute. I suspect this murder investigation has sidelined his proposal plan. For now.

"Let's see what Lucas says," I suggest, trying to calm both of us down.

"The coroner found fibres in Mysti's lungs," Eric says, changing the subject.

"She was definitely smothered, then," I conclude.

Eric nods. "But so far, nothing in the room matches the fibres in Mysti's nose and lungs. They're still processing samples, so hopefully the murder weapon is in the to-be-processed pile." He takes a sip of lemonade. "And I heard from the handwriting expert."

"What did she say?"

"Mysti wrote the note we found in her throat," he confirms. "And forensics confirmed she wrote it with the complimentary note paper and pen from room 107."

"If Mysti wrote the note while she was staying at the Hav-a-nap motel, it was likely intended for someone local," I surmise. "Her killer might be someone we know."

CHAPTER 10

"HE'S PULLING INTO THE DRIVEWAY," Hannah announces, still holding her phone to her ear. "K. See you in a minute. Bye." She hangs up.

Hannah opens the door for Lucas while Eric and I get up from the kitchen table.

"Be nice," I whisper.

"I'll be nice as long as he's honest," Eric mutters in reply.

Lucas stands in the entryway and fidgets with his peaked cap, which is in his hand.

"Chief," he says, nodding at Eric with a tight-lipped smile. "Hi, Megan," he says, the dimple on his right cheek winking at me when he smiles.

Lucas calls Eric "chief" when he's on duty.

"Hi, Lucas." I muster my friendliest tone of voice, hoping to ease his palpable anxiety. "Come in and sit down." I gesture toward the living room. "Can I get you a drink? We have lemonade."

"No, thank you, ma'am." He and Hannah sit next to each other on the sofa, and Sophie joins them, making herself comfortable on Hannah's lap.

Lucas's curly dark hair is damp with sweat either from wearing his dark uniform on a warm day, or because he's nervous, or both.

"Tell them what you told me," Hannah instructs, nudging her boyfriend.

Eric and I sink into the armchairs across from the sofa.

"We're listening," Eric says in his cop voice.

"I was in room 107 at the Hav-a-nap motel on Saturday," Lucas confesses.

"Why didn't you log it?" Eric asks, leaning forward and putting his elbows on his knees, his fingertips touching in front of him.

"I forgot," Lucas admits, sounding disappointed with himself. "I'm sorry. It was near the end of my shift. I guess I was in a hurry to leave, and it slipped my mind. I didn't know about the murder until I clocked in a couple of hours ago. I was going to talk to you later today." He reaches into a pocket and produces a small notebook. "But I have notes." He flips through the pages, then hands the notebook to Eric.

Eric reads the notes, then hands the notebook back to Lucas.

"Tell me everything," Eric instructs. "From the

beginning."

Lucas tells us he was on patrol on Saturday afternoon and pulled into one of the metered parking spots on Water Street, so he could go into a local store to buy a drink. Walking from the car to the store, he heard someone yell, *police.* He says a woman was flagging him down and running toward him.

"What did she look like?" Hannah asks.

I smirk with smug pride at her instinct for focussing on the important details; I like to think she gets it from me.

Lucas describes Mysti to a tee. Right down to the spattering of freckles across her nose.

"She was scared," Lucas says. "I could tell. She was jumpy and kept looking behind her. She said a dissatisfied customer was harassing her, and she thought they were following her."

"Did you see anyone following her?" Eric asks.

"I don't think so," Lucas replies, sounding less than confident. "There was this one guy. I'm not sure if he was following her or just walking fast in the same direction. We made eye contact, and he turned and went the other way. Water Street was busy on Saturday, and I assumed he was trying to get through the crowd." He shrugs. "I pointed him out to Mysti and asked her if he was the guy who was bothering her, but she said it wasn't him."

"What did he look like?" Eric asks, with his own notebook open and his pen in his hand.

"He was younger than you, but older than me. He was taller than me but shorter than you."

This vague description applies to half the men in Harmony Lake.

"What about his hair?" I suggest.

Lucas shakes his head. "I didn't see his hair. He wore a baseball cap. It was black and said, *Dad in charge,* in white letters.

"What else was he wearing?" Eric asks.

"A baby," Lucas replies.

"He was wearing a baby?" Hannah and I ask in stereo.

Lucas looks at Hannah. "Yeah, you know, those baby backpacks that parents wear in the front?" He gestures toward his upper torso to describe the man's baby carrier, then he looks at me. "It was a cute baby." He shrugs one shoulder. "It was facing me. It was smiling, and it's sunhat was too big for its little head."

"Any other identifying features?" Eric asks.

Lucas shakes his head. "No. That's it. I only saw him for a second.

The man Lucas describes sounds like an unlikely suspect. Do killers take their babies when they stalk their victims? I doubt it. First, only a sociopath would take a baby to a murder scene. Second, babies are unknown variables. What if the baby cried, or spat up, or left a clue behind? Or what if the baby was injured? No, this doesn't sound like a solid lead to me, but I'll leave it to the professionals to decide.

"What happened next," Eric probes. "After Mysti flagged you down and told you someone was following her."

"I asked for her name and address." He points to his notebook. "And wrote them down so I could log them later, but I forgot."

"Did you ask to see her ID?" Eric asks.

"Yes, but she didn't have any. I had to take her word for it. I would've run her name when I logged our interaction, but I forgot to log it."

I have a mental flashback to Renée telling me she caught up to Mysti in Harmony Lake because Mysti reused one of her aliases. Oh my! If Lucas had logged his interaction with Mysti, he would've seen that she was wanted in other jurisdictions and taken her into custody. If she were in police custody, instead of her motel room, would Mysti still be alive?

"Tell them the part about the motel," Hannah urges.

"I could tell she was still scared, so I offered to drive her home—to the motel," Lucas reveals. "She accepted my offer. When we arrived, she was antsy and looked around like she expected someone to jump out at her. I offered to clear her room, so she would relax."

"Did you clear the room?" Eric asks.

"Yes," Lucas confirms. "And she was much calmer when I told her it was clear. I offered to help her file a report about the customer who was bothering her, but she didn't want to. She said disgruntled customers take out their frustration on her sometimes. She said it was an occupational hazard. I asked her for a description, and she blew me off, saying it didn't matter."

Eric, Hannah, and I sound like a leaky air mattress as we let out a collective sigh of relief. This explains why Lucas's fingerprints were all over Mysti's motel room; he turned on every light and opened every door to make sure no one was there.

"Then you left?" I ask.

"Yes, but first, I offered to wait while she called someone to come and stay with her," Lucas explains. "She said her roommate would be back soon, and she would be fine." He looks at Eric. "I saw evidence of a male roommate when I cleared the room, so I assumed her husband or boyfriend would be back soon. She went inside, and I left."

"Let's talk about the importance of logging every interaction," Eric says, noticeably more relaxed than he was before Lucas got here.

Again, I offer Lucas a drink, and he accepts a glass of water. Thank goodness. I don't need to sit here while Eric lectures him about work stuff. Hannah follows me into the kitchen.

"I told you he would have a good explanation!" Hannah declares, relieved she was right.

"I didn't doubt it, sweetie," I fib.

"Are you going to tell Dad about this?" she asks. "I don't want him to know. He doesn't need to know. This will give him another reason to hate Lucas."

Until this moment, I wasn't sure if Hannah was aware of Adam's feelings about her boyfriend.

"I won't tell him," I assure her, "but you know what this town is like. Dad will probably hear about it from someone. Wouldn't it be better if one of us tells him?"

"I know, but Dad will use it as an excuse to hate Lucas. He'll say Lucas is a suspect until the police arrest someone else."

She's not wrong; she knows her dad well.

"I can be there when you tell him," I offer. "It's up to you."

Hannah nods with tears in her eyes. "Thanks," she mumbles.

"Come here, Hannah Banana." I envelop my daughter in a tight hug. We sway, and I smooth her long curls with my hand. "Dad doesn't hate Lucas," I explain while I hold her. "He hates the idea of Lucas. Dad is used to being the number one man in your life. He loves you so much that he thinks no one could ever love you as much as him. He'll come around," I assure her.

"But until the police charge someone else with Mysti's murder, Lucas is a suspect," Hannah says when we pull apart. "He slept in yesterday. Remember? He was late picking me up to go apartment hunting. Mum, he doesn't have an alibi for when Mysti was killed."

I brush a stubborn curl from her face and tuck it behind her ear.

"Then we'll have to find Mysti's killer and make sure they're held accountable."

CHAPTER 11

"Bye, Lucas," I say, as he steps out of the house.

"I'll be right back," Hannah beams. "I'll just walk Lucas to the car."

Eric and I nod. Sophie leaps onto the back of the living room sofa, so she can watch Hannah and Lucas on the driveway.

"What do you think?" I ask when the door closes.

"The poor guy. He's wracked with guilt," Eric says.

"About what?" I ask, wondering if Lucas realized running Mysti's alias through the computer might've saved her life.

"He's convinced whoever was following Mysti came back for her after he left."

"He might be right," I suggest. "If Lucas ran Mysti's name through the computer, would she have been in police custody when her killer went to her room?"

"Unlikely," Eric says. "She didn't have a record. And

they wanted to question her, not charge her." He shrugs. "We would've processed her, then released her. She would've been back at the motel by dinnertime."

"Renée Dukes was surveilling Mysti on Saturday," I say. "April and I saw her on a park bench near Mysti's fortune-telling blanket. If Mysti had an altercation, or ran away, Renée should've seen what happened. But she didn't mention it when April and I talked to her." Renée's story and role in Mysti's case aggravates the knot in my stomach. I don't trust her. "Maybe Renée was the person who was chasing Mysti."

"Didn't Lucas say Mysti was running from a man?" Eric asks, with his gaze focused down and to the left; his favourite gaze for thinking.

"Did Lucas say it was a man, or did we *assume* it was a man because he saw the dad with the baby walking fast behind Mysti?"

"I'll talk to Lucas and clarify," he says. "Do you believe Lucas's story?"

"I have to," I reply with a sigh. "Hannah believes him, and she needs me to trust her instincts about him. She already knows Adam doesn't like him. She needs one parent to support her."

"I get it, babe," Eric responds. "It's stressful for older, established couples to cope with one of them being a person of interest in a murder investigation, never mind a young couple in a new relationship."

"I need Adam to adopt that point of view," I say. "Is the baby-wearing dad a good lead?"

"I'd like to talk to him," Eric replies. "If he wasn't following Mysti, maybe he saw who was."

"Mysti must have been terrified, Eric," I say. "She told Jax she didn't want to go to the police because she was afraid they would arrest her, but she flagged down Lucas for help. Mysti took a big risk when she approached him. She'd only do it if she was desperate."

"I know." He hugs me and rubs circles on my back. "I have to go to work. Can I show you something before I go?"

"Sure," I reply.

Eric opens his phone and shows me a photo. It's a selfie of Mysti and another woman. They're about the same age. Their arms are around each other's shoulders. Both women are mid-laugh and look like they might be intoxicated.

"Where did you get this?" I ask.

"We recovered it from Mysti's burner phone," he says. "She took them last week."

"Them?" I ask. "There's more?"

He nods.

"May I?" I ask before I swipe to the next photo.

"Of course," he replies. "They took the photos at the same time and place. Every photo has the same background, and their clothing doesn't change. I suspect they were drinking."

I swipe through the photos. Mysti and her friend make faces for the camera. They look like they're having fun, and I can't help but smile at their exaggerated facial expressions. The photos are a tad blurry, adding to my hunch that the ladies in the photos were inebriated. They remind me of April and I; we sometimes take silly selfies after a few glasses of wine. The background is familiar. I zoom in on one familiar head in particular.

"This is The Embassy," I say, handing the phone with the zoomed-in photo to Eric. "That's Sheamus."

The Irish Embassy—known to the locals as The Embassy—is our local Irish Pub. Sheamus is the owner. His full head of brilliant ginger hair makes him stand out in the background, even if he is blurry.

"You're right," he agrees, taking the phone and inspecting the background on the other photos. "Do you recognize the woman in the photos with Mysti?"

"No," I reply. "But if you send me the least blurry picture, I'll ask around and keep an eye out for her."

Unless this mystery woman is slightly blurry and makes duck lips in person, I'm not sure I'd recognize her, but I'll keep my eyes open.

"Thanks." Seconds later, my phone dings when he texts me the picture. "I'll send someone to The Embassy to ask around and look for her."

"Jax might know who she is," I suggest. "He was Mysti's roommate, after all."

"I'll ask him when he gets back from his interview."

Eric kisses me goodbye and passes Hannah at the door on his way out.

"How do you feel?" I ask, rubbing Hannah's arm.

"I'm OK," she replies with a sigh. "Lucas is upset. He feels like Mysti might not be dead if he pushed her harder to talk about who was following her, and if he ran her name through the computer."

"Eric said even if Lucas arrested her, it wouldn't have changed Mysti's outcome," I assure her.

Hannah nods. "I know. He said the same thing to Lucas. But he still wonders *what if,* you know?"

"How was your shift at the library this morning?" I ask.

"Fine," she says, shrugging. "Kind of slow. People do outdoor activities when the weather is good."

"How was Mrs. Bickerson?" I specify.

"Not her usual cheery self," Hannah admits. "She and Kilian stayed in her office with the door closed. Mrs. B never closes her office door. It goes against her open-door policy."

"Mrs. B was close with Mysti," I explain. "Mysti's death might be hard for her."

"I know," Hannah tells me. "The other summer interns said Mrs. B told everyone who came to the library last week how amazing Mysti was. She praised Mysti's gift and tried to convince everyone to see her." Hannah fidgets with her hands like she's trying to figure out what to say next. "Mum, I think Mrs. B might know something about what happened to Mysti."

"Did you tell Eric?" I ask.

She shakes her head. "I was going to, but the situation with Lucas's fingerprints made me forget. I didn't remember until now when you asked about Mrs. B."

"Why do you think Mrs. B knows something?"

"Because when she left her office to take Kilian outside, she was crying. I took some tissues and followed her outside. When I handed her the tissues, she thanked me and I asked her if she was OK. She said she was fine, but *poor Mysti was right about the woman coming to get her*."

"Were those her exact words?"

Hannah nods. "Yes. I should tell Eric, right?"

"For sure," I reply. "Send him a text. Tell him what you told me."

That's the rest of my day sorted. If anyone needs me, my crochet hook and I will be binge-watching Netflix and finishing a few lap blankets, so I can drop them off at the library tomorrow and visit Mrs. Bickerson.

CHAPTER 12

TUESDAY, June 15th

"Wow! That's a lot of mail, Soph," I say as Sophie innocently traipses across the scattered envelopes on her way into the store.

I stoop down and pick up yesterday's mail off the floor. There's more than usual. I sign up for electronic correspondence and opt out of snail mail whenever possible. We never get this much physical mail anymore.

Knitorious has a new postal carrier. On Mondays, she pushes the mail through the mail slot in the front door. I'm not complaining, it's her job. But I miss our old carrier, who held on to Monday's mail and delivered it the next day with Tuesday's mail.

Flipping through the envelopes, it becomes clear why there's so much; I have mail for three other Water Street stores. *Sigh.* I sort the non-Knitorious mail into piles and set them aside. I'll deliver them to their intended destinations when Hannah starts her shift at lunchtime.

Just after I flip the sign from CLOSED to OPEN and unlock the door, Hannah arrives.

"What are you doing here?" I ask. "You don't start until noon."

"I told Eric I'd take Sophie to the dog park," she replies, squatting down to rub Sophie, who's super excited to see her.

"I already walked Sophie," I say. "We had a nice leisurely stroll before I opened the store."

"I promised, so I feel like I should take her."

"Why does Sophie have to visit the dog park every day?" I demand. "She coped just fine when we only took her a few times a week. Why, all of a sudden, does she have to go every day?"

Hannah shrugs. "She likes it there. She has canine friends that she plays with, and it's part of her routine now."

Am I having déjà vu or is this what Eric said word-for-word yesterday when I asked him the same question?

"Did Eric tell you to say that?"

"Pretty much," Hannah admits, picking up two of Sophie's toys and getting her leash.

"Good morning!" Jax appears in the doorway between the store and the back room.

Hannah and I greet him and ask how he's doing. He

tells us he's fine, and we exchange pleasantries about the wonderful weather we've been enjoying.

"How was your interview yesterday?" I ask.

"I think it went well," Jax replies. "I guess I'll find out for sure if they offer me the job. I have another interview this afternoon. With the Harmony Lake Fire Department."

"I didn't know you applied there," I comment.

"I didn't," Jax responds. "Adam introduced me to the fire chief last night at The Embassy." He shrugs. "Now I have an interview."

The Harmony Lake Fire Department has been one firefighter short of a full roster since January. I assumed they hired someone by now, but I guess not.

"Good luck," I say. "I'm sure they'll love you."

"How did you meet my dad?" Hannah asks.

"Eric had to work late last night on Mysti's case," Jax explains. "I was bored in the apartment by myself, and Eric suggested I go to the pub for dinner. He said it was steak and mushroom boxty night, and his friends would be there watching the game. When I got there, Adam recognized me and waved me over. I sat with him and a bunch of other guys. The fire chief was there, and Adam told him about my training."

I didn't give Adam details about Jax's training or job search. He and Eric devised this scheme on their own. I suspect Eric hopes Jax will settle in or near Harmony Lake.

"We'll ask everyone to put in a good word for you," Hannah says.

"Thanks," Jax replies, then looks at me. "Megan, can I ask you a favour?"

"Of course," I reply. "What do you need?"

"Eric said I can go to room 107 and collect my stuff. I don't want to go alone, and Eric has to work. He said you might come with me."

"Sur…"

"I'll go with you," Hannah offers, interrupting me before I finish my sentence. "We're practically step-cousins." She shrugs with a smile. "Can you wait until I get back from the dog park?" She points to Sophie, sitting at her feet, staring at the dog toys in Hannah's hand.

"Can I go to the dog park with you?" Jax asks. "It'll give me something to do other than obsess about my interview."

"Sure!"

"Before you go," I interject, just as Hannah bends down to attach Sophie's leash, "can you watch the store for a few minutes?" I pick up the piles of mis-delivered mail from the counter. "I need to drop off some mail."

"Sure."

"No problem."

"Thanks," I say, grabbing my phone and slipping it in my pocket. "I'll be back soon."

Two down, one to go. After I drop off Wilde Flowers' mail, I can go back to Knitorious.

Wilde Flowers is next door to Knitorious; we share a wall and a parking lot. The owner, Phillip Wilde, is my next-door neighbour at home too. We're work and home neighbours.

"Good morning, Phillip," I say loud enough for him to hear me over the jingle of his door.

"Why, Megan Martel!" He comes out from behind the counter. "To what do I owe this unexpected pleasure?" Phillip bows, his right hand spiralling in front of his chest with a dramatic flourish.

"I come bearing gifts," I say, playing along, "of the postal variety." I slap the envelopes on his counter.

"Again?!" He stands up. "I like the new postal carrier," he says. "She's friendly and chatty and all that good stuff, but she's not very detail oriented, is she?"

I shake my head. "Where's Kevin?" I ask, looking around for Phillip's beloved Chihuahua, expecting to find him perched atop his royal blue velvet pillow with gold piping and tassels. "He's not on his pillow."

Kevin and Phillip are always together. I can't remember the last time Wilde Flowers was open for business and Kevin wasn't here.

"He's at the vet," Phillip replies. "Getting his teeth cleaned. Plaque is a horrible thing, and it gives Kevin the worst halitosis."

"Thank goodness," I say. "I worried for a second." Glancing at the counter, it looks like Phillip was in the middle of ringing up a sale before I interrupted him. "Were you in the middle of something?"

Phillip flicks his wrist. "I'm waiting for a customer to come back. He left his wallet at the park or something. I have time for a quick chat." He smirks and gives me a sideways glance. "What's the latest on the fortune teller's murder?"

"How would I know?" I tease.

"Because you always know."

"I know the police have a lot of suspects and a lot of evidence to sift through," I tell him, hoping to satisfy his curiosity.

"You know more than that," he says. "I'll tell you something juicy if you tell me something juicy," Phillip suggests.

"Deal."

"OK." His eyes light up like a Christmas tree. "According to Trudy, Mrs. Willows said Artie saw Eric coming out of Charmed and Dangerous last week."

Charmed and Dangerous is our local jewellery store.

"You call that juicy?" I smirk. "It's fourth-hand gossip at best."

Phillip shrugs. "It's been a slow week for me."

"Eric could've been there for anything," I assert. "It could have been work related. He could've been getting a new battery for his watch…"

"Or an engagement ring," Phillip finishes my sentence. "I sense there's a wedding in our future, sweetie, and I'm already thinking about the flowers.

What do you think your colour scheme will be? In which season will the nuptials take place?"

I feel my face blushing. "Artie is legally blind in four provinces. He probably saw someone who looked like Eric," I say, ignoring Phillip's questions.

"Speaking of people who look like Eric," Phillip probes, "what's the story behind the mini-Eric staying at your apartment?"

"There's nothing mini about Jax," I correct him.

"You can say that again," Phillip agrees with a wink.

"I promise to tell you more about that later this week." I smile.

"You owe me something juicy."

I think hard about what I can tell Phillip that will satisfy his curiosity without compromising the investigation.

"OK," I say, leaning toward Phillip like I'm about to tell him something that will blow his mind. "The fortune teller's true identity is a closely guarded secret, but when it becomes public, her death will make head-lines all over the world."

Wide-eyed, Phillip gasps and brings his hand to his mouth. "Tell me!" He swats my shoulder. "You can't leave me hanging! Who is she?"

Saved by the bell. A man sweeps in, rushing to the counter.

"Sorry about that!" the mystery man says, "but I'm here now." He turns to me. "I'm sorry, were you in the middle of a transaction?" He smiles.

Speechless, I shake my head, unable to stop staring at him or the baby he's wearing in his baby-carrier. A cute, smiling baby whose sun hat is too big for his little head.

The man turns back to Phillip. "I found it," he explains, holding up his wallet. "It was buried in the bottom of the diaper bag." He chuckles, and Phillip joins him.

While Phillip finishes ringing up the mystery man's transaction, I reposition myself to better view the man's hat. A black baseball cap with white letters that say *Dad in charge.*

No way! This is the baby-wearing dad! I need to take a picture and send it to Lucas. But how, without being obvious? Before I can think through my dilemma, Phillip hands him his receipt and wishes him a good day.

"Have a great day," the man says, turning to leave.

"Bye," I mumble.

When the door closes behind him, I rush to the window. He crosses the street and walks toward the park. He veers toward the playground, waving to someone I can't see.

"Who was that?" I demand.

"Some guy who bought flowers for his wife," Philip shrugs. "Pink peonies."

"What's his name?" I clarify.

"I have to protect my client's privacy, Megan."

"Phillip. There's no such thing as florist-customer confidentiality," I reason. "I *need* to know his name."

He narrows his eyes. "Does it have anything to do with the fortune teller's murder?"

I nod.

"In that case, his name is Cole Duffy with two f's. His wife's name is Kelsi with an i. They aren't local. They have a vacation rental until the middle of July. He paid with cash."

I pull out my phone and make a quick note of the names.

"Thank you, Phillip!" I say, shoving my phone in my pocket. "I have to go."

"If you wait ten minutes, I'll be finished with your June arrangement, and you can take it with you."

"I'll come back for it," I call on my way to the door.

"It's OK, I'll drop it off later." His voice grows fainter as the door closes behind me.

CHAPTER 13

"C'MON, SOPH!" I blurt out, spying her leash and rushing to snatch it off the counter.

"Mum, what's wrong?" Hannah jumps off the sofa in the cozy seating area.

"The baby-wearing dad is across the street!" I exclaim, attaching the leash to Sophie's collar.

"Are you sure?" she asks.

"Same hat, same baby," I say, leading Sophie toward the door.

"Why do you need Sophie?"

"So I can take his picture without being obvious," I explain. "I'm just a woman walking her dog."

Hannah nods, fast. "We can send it to Lucas to confirm it's him."

"Exactly."

Hannah turns to Jax. "Can you go with her?" she asks. "In case this guy is dangerous?"

"For sure!" Jax rushes to the door.

As we cross the street, I give Jax the short-version explanation of who the baby-wearing dad is and how he might help Eric find Mysti's killer.

"Got it," he says, like I just gave him a life-or-death assignment. "Black hat, cute baby, big sunhat."

"Last I saw, he was headed toward the playground," I say, steering us in the right direction.

"We should slow down," Jax advises. "You look like you're on a mission. It'll draw attention to us."

I nod and take a deep breath.

"Good call," I say, slowing my pace, much to Sophie's relief as she stops to sniff a nearby tree.

This is the first time I've been alone with Jax since Saturday. I should use this opportunity to check in with him.

"How are you doing, Jax?" I ask. "You came to Harmony Lake expecting to find your biological father, and instead, you found an uncle, a murder investigation, and some pretty quirky people."

"Actually, I like it here. Especially the quirky people." His chuckle sounds so much like Eric's it makes me hold my breath for a moment. "Everyone is really nice and accepting of me. People make me feel welcome. Even if I don't develop a relationship with my father, I'm glad Eric is my uncle."

"I think he's glad he's your uncle too," I say. "He's eager to tell people who you are. But he's waiting for the DNA results."

"I know," Jax responds. "Jason isn't as eager. He won't book a plane ticket until the DNA results come back." He sighs. "We only spoke on the phone once, and he didn't ask for my number or email address or anything. But Eric shows me family photos and tells me about my other relatives. He asks me about my life and asks to see my family photos. For brothers who look almost identical, Eric and Jason couldn't be more different."

"I'm sorry Jason isn't as enthusiastic as you hoped," I commiserate. "He might need time to process everything. His wife and other kids might need time too. The rest of the Sloanes will be excited about you, regardless of Jason's reaction. And if Jason never gets used to the idea, it's his loss. You're a great person, and he should be proud you're his son."

He nods. "My dad said the same thing," Jax says, referring to the dad who raised him. "If I ask you something, Megan, will you be honest?"

"I'll do my best," I say, sensing he's about to ask me something serious.

Jax inhales and blows it out. "Do you think I killed Mysti?"

"No," I reply without hesitation, shaking my head.

"You sound sure."

"I am sure," I admit. "I was pretty sure until this morning, but now I'm one hundred percent sure."

"What happened that made you sure?"

"It was when Hannah offered to go to the motel

with you," I explain. "I didn't feel any anxiety or hesitation. If *any* part of me believed there was even a slight chance you did anything to Mysti, my instincts would've kicked in, and I would've panicked about Hannah being alone with you." I shrug. "But my first instinct was that I'm happy you're getting to know each other."

"I didn't hurt Mysti," Jax insists. "I swear on my family's lives. I know her fortune-telling job was a con, and I know she was wrong to trick people, but she didn't deserve what happened to her."

"I agree with you," I say.

"And she wasn't all bad," he adds. "Mysti said most of her clients knew her gift wasn't real. They saw her for entertainment. Mysti's readings cost the same as going to a movie. She also said some sad and broken people went to see her. Mysti said they were grieving and in pain. She tried to tell those people what they needed to hear to bring them comfort and give them peace. So they could move on. A bad person wouldn't do that."

My thoughts instantly turn to Mrs. Bickerson and the sense of comfort she exuded when she told me how Mysti's readings helped her to find peace after her parents' deaths.

As we get closer to the playground, I spot the baby-wearing dad near the monkey bars with a little girl. She's about three, and he hovers nearby, ready to catch her if she falls. A woman, who I assume is his wife, follows a toddler around the perimeter of the whirl spinner. Three kids under four! Cole Duffy and his wife are busy parents!

Jax stops walking and faces the other way.

"What's wrong?" I ask.

"If he sees me, he'll bolt," Jax replies.

"Why?"

"He's the guy who argued with Mysti at the motel on Friday."

"The baby-wearing dad is the man you scared off when you met Mysti?"

"Yup," Jax confirms. "There's no doubt about it. That's him."

Interesting.

A woman is walking a chocolate lab about fifty feet behind us. Jax nods toward the lab.

"I'll hang back here," he suggests. "Close enough to reach you, but too far away for him to see me."

Before I can respond, he's walking toward the lab with his hand out and asking the owner the dog's name. I hear her respond, "Guinness," as Sophie and I walk farther away from Jax and closer to the playground.

I unlock my phone and open the camera. I turn the front-facing camera on and turn my back to the playground, positioning myself until Cole Duffy is on my screen and in focus. Pretending to take a selfie, I snap a few photos of him. With my back still toward the playground, I open the photo app to ensure the photos are usable and clear enough that Lucas will recognize the baby-wearing dad. They're perfect.

I open the text app, and I'm about to send the photos to Eric when I'm interrupted by a tiny voice behind me.

"Excuse me, may I please pet your dog please?"

Cole Duffy and his daughter are less than two feet away from me. The little girl is adorable, and when she says please twice, I almost melt from the cuteness.

"Absolutely," I say, smiling.

While I shorten Sophie's leash and tell her to sit down, Cole praises his daughter for using her good manners when she asked to pet Sophie.

"Her favourite spot is between her ears," I tell the little girl as I crouch down next to Sophie and grip her collar.

Sophie is a good girl. She loves people—kids are her favourite kind of people—and she's the gentlest dog you'll ever meet. But just in case, I always stay extra close and have extra control when new people approach her.

"What's her name?" the tiny voice asks.

"Sophie," I reply.

Cole Duffy shows his daughter how to close her hand and extend it for Sophie to sniff before petting her. By the time the tiny hand touches her, Sophie is practically vibrating with anticipation.

"Good girl, Soph," I whisper to the patient corgi.

And just like that, the little girl decides she's

finished petting Sophie, turns around, and hightails it back toward the playground.

"What do you say, Pumpkin?" Cole calls after the tiny escapee.

"Thank you," the tiny voice calls, sounding even tinier because she's running away.

"Thank you for your patience," Cole says. "To you and Sophie." He rubs Sophie between the ears.

"Your kids are adorable," I say, smiling at the kicking baby who's grinning at me from the baby carrier on Cole's chest.

"Thanks!" He smiles. "There's one more,"—he points toward the playground—"over there with her mum."

"Is that your wife?" I ask, nodding toward the woman trying to follow a toddler and a preschooler in different directions.

"That's her," he confirms.

"You have a beautiful family."

"Yes, I do," he agrees. "But at their current ages, it's a handful."

"I can only imagine," I say, distracted by the adorable baby cooing at me and reaching for me with his chubby hands.

"I'm Cole, by the way." He smiles and extends his hand.

"Megan." I smile and shake his hand.

"Do you have kids?" he asks.

"One," I reply, holding up my index finger. "My

daughter is an adult now. I'm about seventeen years ahead of you."

"Well, it's nice to meet someone who made it through this parenting gig and came out the other side. It gives me hope my wife and I will survive."

We laugh.

"You're not local, are you?" I ask. "If you were local, we would've crossed paths before."

"We're vacationing here for another month," Cole confirms. "We're renting a lakeside cottage. It's a beautiful town."

"Yes, it is," I agree. "I hope the murder on Sunday at the local motel didn't lower your opinion of us." I'm trying to introduce Mysti's murder without being confrontational.

"Not at all," Cole responds. "It's tragic, but these things can happen anywhere. I heard she was a transient with a shady fortune-telling gig. She probably pissed off lots of people."

Not very sympathetic, Cole.

"Are you one of those people?" I ask.

He scrunches up his face and shifts his gaze from side to side, like my question is preposterous.

"Why would you ask that?"

"Because one person saw you arguing with Mysti and another saw you chasing her on Water Street." So much for avoiding confrontation!

"I never met that woman." He shrugs and shifts his weight from one foot to the other while giving the baby a gentle bounce. The baby giggles with glee. Cole narrows his eyes. "Are you a cop or something?"

I shake my head. "No." I smile. "Just a concerned resident."

"Look." He takes a deep breath and turns his head, checking our surroundings. "I had words with the fortune teller, OK?"

"Words about what?" I inquire.

"We were at the beach last week, and the fortune teller offered my wife a reading," Cole explains. "My wife wasn't interested, but the fortune teller wouldn't leave her alone. She kept pressuring her to get a reading. Kept lowering her price, stuff like that. We were trying to spend quality time together as a family, but she wouldn't take no for an answer. I finally told her to back off."

"This happened at the beach?" I confirm.

"Yeah," he insists. "It was a weekday, and it wasn't very busy. I don't know if anyone witnessed it."

"Wow," I say. "Thanks for clearing that up, Cole. I hope the rest of your vacation is less eventful."

He turns to check on his wife and other children.

"I have to go. My wife is outnumbered over there."

"Bye, Cole. It was nice to meet you," I say as he rushes away. "Ready, Soph?" I ask, steering us toward Jax.

Jax and his new best friend, Guinness, are playing fetch while Guinness's owner sits on a nearby bench, chatting with a friend.

"How'd it go?" Jax asks as Sophie and I approach him.

"Interesting," I reply.

Sophie and Guinness greet each other the way dogs do. When Guinness's owner whistles, he picks up his tennis ball and obediently trots over to her.

"Bye, Guinness." Jax waves at the chocolate lab. "Bye, ma'am." He waves at the owner, who waves back.

"He mentioned nothing about being at the Hav-a-nap motel," I tell Jax.

"He was there," Jax insists. "And he was angry."

"He lied to me at least once."

"How do you know?" Jax asks.

"He contradicted himself," I reply. "First, he said he never met Mysti, then he admitted he had words with her on the beach."

"Did you get his picture?"

I snap my fingers. I forgot about the picture!

"Yes," I reply, stopping to open my phone and text the photos to Eric.

Me: Found the baby-wearing dad! Cole Duffy is at the playground on Water Street right now.

Eric: Thanks, babe! Followed by a red heart emoji.

While the photo app is open, I show Jax the selfie of Mysti and her friend.

"Did Eric show you this?" I ask, handing him my phone.

We resume walking toward Knitorious.

"Yeah," Jax says, nodding. "I don't know her, but I think it's Happy Hour."

"You think they took the photo during happy hour at The Embassy?" I clarify.

"No," Jax replies. "I think the mystery woman in the photo is Mysti's friend, Happy Hour."

"Her name is Happy Hour?" I ask, incredulous that a sane parent would name their child Happy Hour.

"I don't think it's her actual name," Jax explains. "I think Mysti couldn't remember her name, so she just called her Happy Hour." He shrugs like this is a reasonable explanation.

"Did she tell you about Happy Hour?"

"A little," he replies. "Mysti met her at the pub one night, and they got drunk together. She said Happy Hour was breaking up with her boyfriend. They drank to take her mind off it. Mysti said Happy Hour's boyfriend was a jerk, and Karma would give him what he deserved."

Was breaking up could have multiple meanings. Did Mysti mean Happy Hour just broke up with her boyfriend? Past tense. Or did she mean Happy Hour was about to break up with her boyfriend? Future tense. I wonder what Happy Hour's boyfriend did to warrant Mysti calling him a jerk and wishing karmic comeuppance on him.

"Did Mysti ever see Happy Hour again?" I ask. "Did they stay in touch?"

"She didn't say," Jax responds. "She said Happy

Hour was in town visiting her boyfriend." He shrugs. "I assumed the boyfriend lives in Harmony Lake, but Happy Hour doesn't."

For the rest of the walk back to Knitorious, I wrack my brain trying to remember if I've heard any recent break-up rumours about anyone local. Nothing comes to mind.

CHAPTER 14

THIS FEELS like the millionth lap blanket I've crocheted together. Two charity knitters brought me enough squares for two more blankets. At this rate, every book lover in the world will have a lap blanket, not just Harmony Lake.

"Is this beautiful bouquet from Eric?" Mrs. Vogel asks.

"Yes," I reply, smiling. "It's my June floral arrangement. Phillip delivered it while Sophie and I were at the park earlier."

"How thoughtful and romantic of him," Mrs. Vogel says.

"Yes," I agree, assuming she means Eric, not Phillip.

On one of our first dates, Eric and I attended a fundraiser with a silent auction. One of the silent auction items was a year's worth of floral arrangements. Eric had the winning bid, and each month for twelve months, I received one of Phillip's gorgeous floral creations. Earlier this year, on our first anniversary, Eric renewed the floral deliveries, so now I'm midway through the second year of monthly flowers.

"I hope Hannah gets back soon," Mrs. Roblin says.

"She shouldn't be long," I say. "She's running an errand with Jax."

"We never get to see her anymore since she lives in Toronto most of the year," Mrs. Vogel comments.

"I know," I agree. "I miss her when she's not here."

The ladies knit in silence, making more squares for me to assemble into lap blankets, and I hook in silence, trying to assemble blankets as fast as the charity knitters produce new squares.

The jingle over the door interrupts the soothing, rhythmic clicking of their needles.

"Eric!" Mrs. Roblin declares, placing her knitting in her lap. "What an unexpected, pleasant surprise."

If I didn't know better, Mrs. Roblin's enthusiasm would lead me to believe a rock star just walked into Knitorious.

Eric smiles. "Good afternoon, ladies." He hands me an iced vanilla latte.

"Thank you," I mutter with a smile.

Eric doesn't look right. His hair is mussed, and he didn't shave today. He hates being unshaven.

"If I'd known you would be here, I would have

brought you some cabbage rolls," Mrs. Vogel says with a hint of disappointment. "Eric loves my cabbage rolls," she says, smiling and looking at Mrs. Roblin.

"Yes, you keep saying," Mrs. Roblin responds with polite curtness.

The charity knitters *love* Eric. In private, I call them his fan club. They love to feed him and, for reasons unknown, believe he requires a constant supply of food he cannot obtain for himself.

"That's very kind of you, Mrs. Vogel, but I just had a sandwich." He grins at her, tapping his finger on the counter and shifting his weight from one foot to the other.

"Next time," she responds.

"I can't wait," Eric says in a tone that I know is sarcastic but seems to encourage the charity knitters. He looks at me. "Can I talk to you for a minute, babe?"

We ignore the quiet, simultaneous *aww* sounds coming from Mrs. Roblin and Mrs. Vogel.

Waiting for my response, Eric rubs the back of his neck and rocks on his heels. He's not his usual composed self. He's twitchy and can't stay still. Something's going on.

"Well," I hem and haw. "I can't leave the store right now. Today is Stitch-Fix. I need to be here in case a knitter shows up."

On Tuesday afternoons, Knitorious hosts Stitch-Fix, a clinic for knitters to bring in their knitting problems and mistakes so Connie and I can help fix them. Some Tuesdays are so busy we get more knitting issues than we can fix in one afternoon, and other weeks only one or two knitters bring in their knitterly frustrations.

"We'll watch the store, Megan," Mrs. Roblin offers. "Mrs. Vogel and I have yet to encounter a knitting problem we can't solve."

"You can say that again," Mrs. Vogel says with a giggle. "Between us, we have over a hundred years of knitting experience."

Wow. I've never thought of it like that.

"Are you sure?" I ask. "I don't want to impose or interrupt your own knitting."

"Go!" Mrs. Roblin shoos us away with her hand. "Take all the time you need."

Eric and I thank them and retreat to the upstairs apartment.

"What's up?" I ask my jittery boyfriend.

"Nothing," Eric replies, kissing me hello. "Why? Do I look like something's up? I just want to ask you about your encounter with Cole Duffy."

While Eric paces and nods, I tell him about my conversation with Cole Duffy.

After my statement, Jax returns to the apartment. He's wearing a hiking backpack, and he's lugging a huge rucksack.

"Hannah's downstairs with the knitting ladies," he says. "One of them asked me twice if I like cabbage rolls as much as Eric."

"Unless you like them a lot, tell her you have a cabbage allergy," Eric suggests, grinning.

Eric doesn't like cabbage rolls very much, but he eats one in front of Mrs. Vogel whenever she gives him some because he doesn't want to disappoint her. He does this with all the food his fan club gives him, even food he doesn't like. Wouldn't it be hilarious if Mrs. Vogel hates making cabbage rolls and only makes them because she thinks Eric loves them?

"I'm going to unpack and do my laundry," Jax says, then disappears into the spare bedroom.

"Did you find Cole Duffy at the park?" I ask, returning to our previous conversation.

"Uh-huh," Eric replies, pacing around the living room. "He was with his wife and kids. He's going to the station when their kids go down for a nap." The red veins in his eyes are more prominent than usual.

"Do you think he'll show up?" I ask, trying to determine if he's under-slept, over-caffeinated, or both.

The good news is this incarnation of Eric—jittery and exhausted—means we're about halfway through the investigation. This happens when he has lots of pieces of the investigative puzzle and is trying to figure out how they fit together.

"I know he will," Eric says with a confident chuckle. "He's terrified his wife will find out we want to talk to him. He'll show up so we won't go looking for him."

Wouldn't Cole *want* the police to talk to his wife? If he was honest with me about his altercation with Mysti,

Cole's wife would have witnessed it and can verify his story.

Eric sits next to me and rubs his stubbled chin.

"How much coffee have you had?" I ask.

"Today?"

I nod.

He shrugs. "I don't know." He smiles. "It's not like I write it down, babe."

Eric has two cups of coffee. Every day. No more, no less. Always before noon. Dark roast, double-double.

"Did you sleep last night?"

"Of course, I slept," he scoffs.

"How long?"

"Almost two hours," he says, like it's an achievement.

Eric is brought to us today by not enough sleep and too much caffeine.

"Tell me what happened last night."

He groans. "It was that selfie from Mysti's phone." He leans back and laces his fingers behind his head. "Something about it bothered me, but I couldn't put my finger on it. Every time I closed my eyes, I saw that picture."

"The selfies you showed me of Mysti and Happy Hour?"

He nods. "I finally realized why it bothered me."

"What was it?" I'm enthralled.

"Mysti's shirt," he replies, unlocking his phone and

handing it to me with the duck-lipped selfie of the two young women on the screen. "It was missing."

I look at the photo, paying particular attention to Mysti's shirt, a blush coloured, cap-sleeved boatneck. The selfies only show Mysti and her friend from the chest up, so I can't see the bottom half of their outfits, but judging from these photos, there's nothing extraordinary about Mysti's shirt.

"Mysti's shirt was missing?" I ask, making sure I understand.

"It wasn't with the rest of her stuff, and she wasn't wearing it when she died," Eric clarifies, sitting up. "Mysti was a light traveller. She had a small wardrobe. We collected and catalogued all her belongings. The shirt wasn't there. It was driving me nuts, so I went to room 107."

"What time?" I ask.

"Just after midnight?" he says with a facial expression that tells me he's not sure.

"Was her shirt in room 107?"

"No," Eric replies. "I looked everywhere. I even searched Jax's stuff in case her shirt got mixed up with his things. Nothing."

"But you found the shirt somewhere?"

He nods. "In a garbage can outside. Turns out, it's not a shirt. It's a dress. One of those long, flowy dresses like the ones you like to wear."

"You went through the garbage?" I ask, scrunching my nose. "Eww."

"It's not always a glamorous job, babe."

Confused, I shake my head. "I think I'm missing something. Why is the shir—dress significant?"

"Why would she throw it away?" he asks, answering my question with a question. "Mysti had a very limited wardrobe. And why use a garbage can outside when there were two garbage cans inside the room?"

"I don't know," I say, shaking my head. "Was the dress torn? Did it have a stain?"

"No, and no," he replies, smirking and leaning in closer. "I don't think Mysti put the dress in the garbage can. I think the killer did after they used it to kill her and exit the motel room without leaving fingerprints."

"You think the dress is the murder weapon?" This blows my mind.

He nods. "I think it's possible. At the very least, I suspect the killer used it to exit the room without leaving fingerprints behind. The coroner found fibres in Mysti's lungs. We know the killer smothered her. But we haven't found anything in the room that matches the fibres."

"So, part of your jitteriness is because you're on pins and needles waiting for the forensic report to confirm the dress is the murder weapon," I deduce.

Eric's eyes light up with relief. "You got it."

"Is it possible the killer left their DNA on the dress?" I ask.

"Maybe," he replies. "It's possible but not probable that they left touch DNA."

Touch DNA is the term for the microscopic skin cells we leave behind when we touch almost anything. Science has evolved to where they can extract these tiny samples and analyse them.

"Babe,"—Eric takes my hand and rubs his thumb in circles on the back of it—"the dress is a hold back."

"Got it," I say, nodding.

A holdback is evidence only the killer, or someone who was at the crime scene, would know about. Police use holdback evidence to eliminate false confessions—a false confessor wouldn't know about the holdback evidence—and to verify the killer. If the killer mentions the holdback evidence, it confirms they were at the crime scene.

"You need a good night's sleep," I say, "in your own bed."

"What about Jax?" Eric asks. "Babe, I want to come home, but I don't want to leave him. What if his DNA results come back, and he's alone?"

"Jax is an adult," I remind him. "We'll invite him to either stay in our spare room or stay here. Either way, he'll be fine. You won't. You need sleep. What if you make a mistake because you're overtired, and it compromises the investigation?"

Eric looks at the ceiling and sighs. "You're right." He squeezes my hand. "I have to talk to Jax about your walk to the park and ask him where he wants to stay.

Then I'll go to the station to interview Cole Duffy. After that, I'll come home."

"Good," I say, leaning into him. "I miss you."

"I miss you too," he says, then kisses the top of my head. "This apartment doesn't feel like home anymore. Home is where you are."

CHAPTER 15

"You're knitting?!" I clutch my chest dramatically as if I'm having a heart attack.

"Don't make a big deal out of it, Mum." Hannah rolls her eyes. "I know how to knit."

"I know you *can* knit. I just haven't seen you do it since you were twelve."

"Thirteen," she corrects me.

"And she's doing a marvellous job," Mrs. Vogel interjects. "Hannah is helping us make lap blanket squares." She smiles.

"Looks like I'll have more lap blankets to assemble." I grin.

"Can I relieve you, Mrs. Roblin?" I ask.

Mrs. Roblin is helping a stitch-fix knitter fix a mystery hole in a sock-in-progress.

"No, thank you, Megan," Mrs. Roblin replies with a giggle. "I'm quite enjoying this." The knitter she's helping looks at her like she just said she quite enjoys eating mud.

"And I got to help someone pick up stitches," Mrs. Vogel boasts. "It was lace so not as easy as you'd think."

"Thank you, ladies." I smile.

"We know we aren't Connie, but we're happy to help you until she gets back," Mrs. Roblin says. "In fact, we'll come back every Tuesday until Connie gets back from Europe."

"I appreciate it," I say, trying not to tear up from their kindness.

"Tell your handsome young man that next week I won't forget the cabbage rolls," Mrs. Vogel adds.

"I will," I promise.

"We might be helpful in other ways," Mrs. Roblin adds with a wink, leaving her knitter to resume knitting now that the mystery hole has been fixed.

"How do you mean?" I ask.

"Well, Connie holds down the fort while you pursue your... *hobby*," Mrs. Roblin replies. "And we cleared our schedules to come to Knitorious any day you need us. So, you can pursue your *hobby* without worrying about the store."

"I'm sorry, I don't understand," I say, shaking my head. "My hobby is knitting."

We're talking about different things. What other hobby do I pursue and leave Connie to hold down the fort at Knitorious? *Hobby* is a euphemism for something. But I don't know what.

"Your *other* hobby." Mrs. Vogel touches my arm and gives me an exaggerated wink.

"They mean the sleuthing, Mum," Hannah interjects. "You know when you talk to people and help Eric solve crimes?"

I look at Mrs. Roblin and Mrs. Vogel. Both women nod and smile.

"Oh," I say. "I guess I've never considered it a hobby."

"Call it whatever you want," Mrs. Roblin says. "Harmony Lake needs a murderer off our streets, and you and Eric are good at doing that."

"The charity knitters have your back and will do whatever necessary to help you and Eric clean up the streets," Mrs. Vogel adds.

She makes it sound like we're trying to bring down a drug cartel.

"You can't be chained to the store when there's a murder to solve," Mrs. Roblin explains. "We need you pounding the pavement, doing whatever it is you do."

"We promised Connie we would keep our collective eye on you while she's away and accommodate your hobby if you need us," Mrs. Vogel adds.

"I think I understand," I respond, hoping this conversation is almost over because looking back and forth between the two women is making me dizzy. "Thank you for explaining it to me." I smile. "And I thought you only came in today to drop off squares and knit."

Mrs. Roblin and Mrs. Vogel giggle.

"There's always more to us than meets the eye, Megan," Mrs. Roblin teases in a way that sounds kind of ominous.

There's an undercurrent of truth to her joke. The charity knitters are an organized network of matriarchs from established Harmony Lake families. They wield a lot of power and influence in the community and use their influence to protect our small town and ensure that Harmony Lake remains... harmonious. The charity knitters helped to convince Adam to run for mayor. They've taken on and defeated big-box corporations who tried to bully their way into our lakeside haven and have caused more than one real estate developer to run away with their tails tucked between their legs.

The Charity Knitting Guild has a complex organizational structure with the older, more mature women holding the highest positions while recruiting and training the next generation to take their place. I suspect Mrs. Roblin is their queenpin, but I'm not sure. They're secretive about who holds what role. Connie is a member of the Charity Knitting Guild, but I'm not. Connie tries to include me and convince me to get involved. The charity knitters meet at Knitorious every Wednesday afternoon to knit, plan future charity projects, and order supplies, so I'm often privy to their coded conversations, but have no idea what they mean. Kind of like the conversation I just had with Mrs. Roblin and Mrs. Vogel about my *hobby*.

"Aren't you handsome!" Mrs. Roblin declares, bringing her hands together in front of her chest.

"He looks just like Eric!" Mrs. Vogel proclaims. "He's the spitting image!"

Intimidated by their enthusiasm, Jax inches into the store from the backroom. He's interview-ready in a suit. His hair is parted and neat. The Sloane genes are so strong, if someone told me Eric's doppelganger time-travelled here from twenty years ago, I'd believe them.

"Ready for your interview?" I ask.

"I think so," he replies, nodding. "But I'm nervous."

"You'll be fine," Hannah assures him.

"I hope so," Jax says, taking a deep breath.

"Trust us, Jax," Mrs. Roblin says. "You'll be fine." She winks.

Is this interview a formality? Is the outcome already decided? Maybe I was wrong about Eric and Adam plotting to introduce Jax to the fire chief. Maybe the charity knitters were behind it.

WHEN JAX LEAVES for his interview, and the satisfied Stitch-Fix knitter leaves with her repaired, hole-less sock, I check the time on the cash register. Three more hours until closing time. I sigh, trying to figure out if today has been one of the longest or shortest days ever. Somehow, it's both. I was hoping to drop off some lap blankets to Mrs. Bickerson today and check in with her after what Hannah told me yesterday.

I join the charity knitters and Hannah in the cozy sitting area, picking up my crochet hook and the lap blanket I was working on before Eric interrupted us.

"Mum, weren't you going to drop off lap blankets to Mrs. Bickerson at the library today?" Hannah asks as if she can read my mind. "Mrs. Roblin and Mrs. Vogel are here if someone needs knitting help, and I'm here for everything else."

"You should go," Mrs. Vogel adds. "We're all worried about Shanice Bickerson. It's no secret she spent a lot of time with the fortune teller. We hear she's downright despondent because of the girl's murder."

"And from what we hear, Boris Bickerson isn't very sympathetic to his wife's sadness."

I'm glad they use their powers for good.

"You've convinced me," I say, placing my crochet hook and lap blanket on the coffee table and standing up. I collect the bag of completed lap blankets from under the counter and throw my bag over my shoulder. "Text me if you need me."

"Meg!"

My eyes search the courtyard for the source of my name.

"Mayor Martel!" Adam and I exchange a cheek kiss.

"Are you looking for me?" Adam asks, his blue eyes squinting into the afternoon sun.

Harmony Lake Town Hall and The Harmony Lake Public Library are in adjoining buildings. The locals call the area in front of the entrances The Courtyard.

"No," I reply. "I wouldn't just show up at your office without calling first. I know how busy you are."

"I'm never too busy for you, Meg." Adam smiles. "Hannah told me about Lucas," he says, taking my arm and leading me to a shady spot under a nearby tree.

"Good," I respond. "She was scared to talk to you about it."

"I could tell," Adam nods. "She called me last night. I could hear the hesitation in her voice."

"What did you say?" I ask, hoping he didn't mess this up.

"I was supportive," he says. "Thankfully it was over the phone, and she couldn't see me roll my eyes."

I sigh and roll my eyes, but Adam can't see them behind my sunglasses. "Hannah is more perceptive than we give her credit for," I say. "She's quite aware of how you feel about her boyfriend."

"She gets that from you," Adam muses. "Hannah's coming to my place for dinner tonight. We're going to eat pizza and download a new romantic comedy she wants to watch."

"You hate rom-coms," I point out.

"I love our daughter more than I hate sappy,

romantic humour," he admits. "You like rom-coms. You should join us."

"I can't," I fib. "I have plans. And I don't want to interrupt your quality time with Hannah."

He scoffs. "You wouldn't be interfering…"

"But thank you for being supportive of her," I interrupt before he lays out a logical, lawyerly argument convincing me to go, "and tolerating a movie you won't like to take her mind off everything. And while I'm thanking you, thank you for introducing Jax to the fire chief."

"It was a straightforward decision, Meg," Adam replies. "He's a firefighter looking for a job, and our fire department is looking for a firefighter."

Was the introduction a fluke, a plot thought up by Adam and Eric, or did the charity knitters mastermind the entire thing? I'm about to ask him, but he opens his mouth to speak.

"Are you on your way to the town hall?" Adam asks. "I'm leaving for the day, but I can come back…"

"I'm going to the library," I interrupt, pointing to the library entrance. "Lap blankets," I explain, holding up the bag.

"Ah," he says. "Hannah told me Mrs. B was upset about the fortune teller who died."

"She told me the same thing," I admit. "Have you seen Mrs. B lately?" I ask, realizing they work next door to each other, so it's plausible. "How does she seem to you?"

"I haven't seen her," Adam insists. "I keep my distance since her blind dog peed on me."

I snort, trying to muffle an outburst of laughter. "Kilian peed on you?" I explode into laughter at the thought.

"It's not funny, Meg," Adam retorts. "I think he mistook me for a tree. Or maybe a hydrant. It happened right there." He points to a nearby bench. "He just walked over to me and relieved himself. It's amazing how well that dog can balance on two legs."

"What did you do when you saw him peeing on you?" I ask, trying to picture the event in my mind's eye.

"Nothing," Adam replies with a shrug. "By the time I realized what was happening, he was almost finished, so…" He stops talking to force down a chuckle. "If I made a scene, I would've looked like a bully. Someone could've recorded it, and it could've gone viral. I don't want to be known throughout history as the mayor who was mean to a blind, three-legged dog, Meg."

I laugh so hard, my side aches. I grab my side, and Adam takes my elbow while I compose myself. I raise my sunglasses to the top of my head and dab the tears from my eyes.

"Poor Kilian," I mutter between outbursts of laughter.

"Poor Kilian?" Adam mimics me. "How about poor Adam? He peed on the leg of my light grey suit, Meg.

That suit was custom-tailored. And he ruined my lucky shoes."

"They don't sound very lucky," I spit out, overcome by a renewed fit of giggles.

"They were my lucky court shoes." Adam rolls his eyes. "You know, the cognac-brown wingtips I wear when I have court."

I dab my eyes and swallow the urge to laugh. "It sucks that a blind, three-legged dog mistook you for a tree, and you lost your lucky shoes." I snort but manage not to succumb to another fit of laughter. "I'm sorry for laughing."

"It's OK," Adam replies. "Now that I say it out loud, it is kind of funny. And it's worth it to be the person who makes you laugh again."

"Mrs. Bickerson must have been mortified," I say, still dabbing at leftover tears of laughter.

"I don't think she knows," Adam replies. "She was bickering with Boris, and they didn't seem to notice. I wasn't about to interrupt their money argument to point out that their dog just ruined my custom-tailored suit and expensive leather shoes."

"How do you know they were arguing about money?" I ask, my interest piqued.

"I heard them. They were only six feet from me. They were so into it they forgot they were in the middle of The Courtyard."

"What did they say?"

"He told her she needed to rein in her spending,"—

he puts air quotes around *rein in her spending*—"then, he said he'd *rather go to jail for killing the trickster than go to the poorhouse because you wasted our money on a scam*." He mimics Mr. B's voice and uses air quotes again.

"Sounds serious," I agree. "When was this?"

"Last week," Adam replies. "Friday. I remember because I used to wear my light grey suit on Fridays, but now I'm considering something more casual. Golf pants and golf shirt."

"Good call," I concur. "You're more approachable when you don't wear a suit."

While Adam contemplates his Friday wardrobe options, I wonder if the trickster Mr. Bickerson was referring to was Mysti and if his threat was serious or if he was just blowing off steam.

CHAPTER 16

"MRS. BICKERSON WILL SEE you in her office." The summer intern points down a long hallway and smiles.

I thank the intern and take a deep breath, hoping one day Mrs. Bickerson will forgive me for what I'm about to do—ask if she thinks her husband could be a murderer. If I'm lucky, one day she'll even speak to me again.

I knock lightly and wait. No response. I crack open the door and peek in. Mrs. Bickerson is at her desk with her head in her hands. I open the door enough to poke my head inside.

"Come in, Megan." Mrs. Bickerson summons me with a wave.

Her closed-mouth smile is tight, and her eyes are puffy and red.

"Hi, Mrs. B," I say softly, sitting across from her and

trying not to stare at the small mountain of wadded up tissues in front of her.

"Hi, Kilian." The dog rests his only front paw on my knee while I rub the top of his head. Recalling Adam's recent experience with Kilian, I wrap my dress around my legs and tuck my feet under my chair, as far from Kilian's line of fire as possible. "Who's a good boy?"

"Kilian is the best boy," Mrs. Bickerson agrees, her voice thick from crying. "You're a nicer boy than your daddy, aren't you, Kilian?" She sniffles. "Yes, you are."

I get the impression Mysti's death isn't the only thing Mrs. Bickerson is crying about today.

Kilian wanders back to his dog bed in the corner, and I unclench my legs, letting them relax into a more natural position.

"I'm sorry about Mysti," I say, and watch tears well up in Mrs. Bickerson's eyes. She nods and pulls a fresh tissue from the box to dab her eyes. "Is there something else going on?" I ask. "Aside from Mysti?"

"Boris," she says with a frustrated groan. "As usual." Her voice hitches on the last word. "Oh, Megan, he was awful," Mrs. Bickerson warbles, her voice almost unintelligible because of the sobs. I place a gentle hand on top of her hand. "Do you want to talk about it?"

"Do you know what Boris said when Mysti was murdered?"

"I have no idea," I reply.

"He said, and I quote,"—Mrs. Bickerson pulls

herself up to her full seated height, puts her hands on her hips, and tucks in her chin toward her neck—"*A real psychic would've seen it coming.*" She does a decent impersonation of her husband. "Then he laughed!"

"Oh my," I commiserate. "I'm sorry he wasn't more sensitive to your feelings."

"He was less than insensitive, Megan," Mrs. Bickerson confides, sounding exasperated. "Insensitive I can handle. But I can't handle happiness. He was happy someone murdered that girl. Since we found out, he's been all smug and self-satisfied. Gloating because *at least everyone's money is safe now that she's gone.*" She once again impersonates Mr. Bickerson.

"Everyone reacts to death in their own unique way," I suggest, trying to comfort her.

"I don't think I can stay married to someone who celebrates the death of a fellow human being."

Oh, my. This is beyond the Bickersons usual bickering about day-to-day stuff.

"Have you told Mr. Bickerson how you feel?" I ask, venturing into couples' therapist territory, a place I'm neither comfortable nor qualified to venture into.

She shakes her head. "We haven't said a word to each other since Sunday night."

Sunday night? Mysti's death became public on Monday morning. Mysti's true identity, Everley Leighton Moregard-Davenhill, still isn't public. Eric says he's waiting for direction from her family. Sounds like the Harmony Lake rumour mill was busy on Sunday night.

I have a lot of questions for Mrs. B, but it's obvious she's not in a state to answer them. Mysti's murder and Mr. Bickerson's reaction are too much for her. I can't do anything to bring Mysti back, but I can support Mrs. Bickerson while she works through her issues with her husband.

I take a deep breath.

"Why don't I go back to Knitorious and relieve Hannah," I suggest. "She can help at the library and you can visit Mr. Bickerson and work it out."

"No way." Mrs. Bickerson shakes her head. "If Boris wants to work this out, he knows where I am. He could talk to me instead of going fishing every day. At least I know where I am on his priority list. After fishing. Fishing, then Shanice!"

"Fishing?" I ask. "Off the pier?"

She nods. "Every morning, rain or shine. I thought under the circumstances he might skip a morning, but noooo."

One pier in particular is popular among the locals for fishing. We call it the fishing pier. You'll almost always find six to twelve people fishing there. Regular fishing in the warm months, and ice fishing in the winter months.

"How did you and Mr. Bickerson find out about Mysti?" I ask.

"I overheard two ladies in The Courtyard talking

about it when I left the library on Sunday," she explains. "One of them said her sister was the maid who found Mysti's body."

"You were at the library on Sunday?" I ask. "Isn't the library closed on Sundays?"

"Yes, but I love to be here when it's quiet. And I get a lot done. The library is my happy place. And last Sunday the steam cleaners came to shampoo the carpets. I had to be here to let them in and keep an eye on things."

"Were you here all day?" I ask, wondering where the Bickersons were when Mysti was killed.

"Kilian and I came here after church. After the cleaners left, I met a friend for a late lunch, then came back."

"Mr. Bickerson was fishing?" I presume.

"He doesn't fish on Sundays," Mrs. Bickerson informs me. "After church, he goes home and listens to his podcasts." She wads up her tissue and tosses it on the mountain of tissues in front of her. "He listens to a bunch of stock market and investment podcasts on Sundays."

"Alone?"

As in, with no witnesses to confirm his alibi?

"Yes." She pulls another tissue from the box and comprehension flashes across her face. "I know what you're getting at, Megan. Boris did not kill Mysti."

I say nothing.

"Yes, he hated Mysti," Mrs. Bickerson continues.

"And yes, he's not sad she's dead, but Boris is not a killer. He'd never raise his hand to someone. It's like my mother used to say." Mrs. Bickerson waggles her finger at me. "Shanice! Alligator lay egg, but him no fowl!" she says, manifesting her late mother's Jamaican accent.

"Things aren't always as they seem?" I ask, attempting to translate.

"Exactly." She smiles, seeming to find comfort from invoking her mother's words of wisdom.

"It's no secret that Mr. Bickerson didn't like Mysti," I point out. "Multiple people saw them exchange hostile words." By multiple people, I mean April and I.

"That doesn't mean he harmed her," Mrs. Bickerson defends.

"And at least one person overheard Mr. Bickerson say he'd rather go to jail for murder than to the poor-house, or something along those lines," I say, struggling to recall Adam's exact words.

"He didn't mean it," Mrs. Bickerson responds, not denying he said it. "He was venting." She blows her nose into her tissue. "If the police think Boris killed Mysti, they're barking up the wrong tree. They need to find the woman who was following her." A fresh supply of tears wells up in her eyes, and her chin quivers.

"What woman?" I ask.

"The woman her family hired, Ren—"

We startle when the office door swings open.

CHAPTER 17

Mrs. Bickerson and I recoil when the door slams into the wall with a heavy *bang*, shaking the office walls.

Confused, Kilian jumps off his dog bed and yowls—something between a bark and a howl—then sniffs the air and makes a hasty retreat to the safety of his owner, cowering under Mrs. Bickerson's desk.

"I'm sorry, Mrs. B," the intern sputters. "I told her you were busy."

Renée Dukes positions herself in the doorway, forcing the intern to stay in the hall.

"It's OK, Cecily," Mrs. Bickerson calls to the intern, then stands up behind her desk.

"Should I call security?" Cecily asks from the hallway.

"In fifteen minutes," Mrs. Bickerson responds. "If Ms. Dukes hasn't left the building in fifteen minutes, call the police. Do you hear me, Cecily?"

"Yes, Mrs. B," Cecily's concerned voice responds. "Fifteen minutes. I'll set my watch."

Mrs. Bickerson called Renée, Ms. Dukes. How do they know each other?

"How do you know my name?" Renée asks, looking Mrs. Bickerson up and down and closing the door behind her.

"Our mutual friend told me," Mrs. Bickerson replies, her gaze steady on Renée.

Renée scowls at me.

"Wasn't me," I clarify, pointing to my chest and shaking my head. "We haven't gotten to you yet."

"Someone at your store told me you were here," Renée says, still scowling at me.

I knit my brows together, confused. "You're looking for me?"

"Who else would I be looking for?" She answers my question with a question.

This conversation feels like a competition in confusion.

"You found me," I announce, correcting my posture. "What's so important that you had to burst into someone's office and terrify a young intern?" I glare at her with one brow arched.

"What did you say to the police about our conversation yesterday?" Renée demands.

I shrug. "Nothing that wasn't true. Why?"

"Because whatever you said convinced them to search my motel room and seize my car. Now I can't escape from this backwards little town, and it's your fault."

Backwards little town? You want to be nasty, Renée? Bring it.

"Your legal issues have nothing to do with me," I proclaim, crossing my arms in front of my chest and crossing my legs. "If the police are suspicious, maybe it's because you lie like a cheap watch."

"Lie about what?" Renée challenges.

She takes a step uncomfortably close to me, and her grip on the back of the chair next to me is so tight her knuckles are white. I refuse to let her intimidate me.

"Let's see," I say, getting ready to count her lies on my fingers. "You said you contacted Mysti's family on Saturday night. That was a lie." I push down one finger with my opposite hand. "You said you'd never spoken to Mysti. That was a lie." I push down another finger with my opposite hand. "You left out the part where a terrified Mysti fled the park and flagged down a police officer for help." I push down another finger with my opposite hand. "You probably left that out because you were the person chasing her."

"What are you talking about?" Renée narrows her eyes and turns her head, looking at me sideways.

"On Saturday?" I remind her. "When you were at the park, *surveilling* Mysti, as you put it."

Renée's face clouds with confusion, and she shakes her head.

"If you were watching Mysti, like you claim, you must've seen her pack up her stuff and take off."

Renée shakes her head again.

"Mysti ran along Water Street. She flagged down a cop because she thought someone was following her." I nod upward toward Renée. "You're the only person we know who was following Mysti."

"What time did this happen?" Renée asks.

"You tell me," I reply with an unintentional snort. "You're the detective."

"So, that's where she went," Renée mumbles under her breath, her gaze fixed on the wall.

"Excuse me?" Mrs. Bickerson asks, cocking her ear in Renée's direction. "You said something?"

"I left the park and went to the deli across the street," Renée explains. "I ordered a sandwich and used the washroom. When I got back fifteen minutes later, Ev —Mysti had disappeared. I thought she was trying to lose me."

"You're denying you chased her?" I confirm.

"I never chased Mysti," Renée insists.

"Why should we believe you?" Mrs. Bickerson asks. "You lie like a rug."

"How would you know?" She scoffs at Mrs. Bickerson. "Just because *she* says so?" Renée glances at me like you'd glance at a pile of dog poop when you warn someone to watch their step. "She doesn't know what she's talking about," Renée chortles, sneering at me. "She's a small-town busybody who thinks sleeping with the local police chief makes her a murder investigator."

Ouch! Her comment hurts more than I expect.

"At least I don't forget to TURN THE PAGE OF THE BOOK I'M PRETENDING TO READ!" I shout, standing up and sinking to her level.

Renée steps back and almost touches the office door.

"Or blend in with the crowd by WEARING THE BRIGHTEST COLOURS I CAN FIND." I gesture to her lime-green, short-sleeved, capris jumpsuit, which is actually super cute, but I'm angry and hurt and want her to feel the same. "Worst PI ever," I mutter under my breath, and sit down again with a huff.

"I knew who you were when I approached you outside the post office, you know!" Renée rolls her eyes.

Is she telling the truth, or trying to make it look like she confided in the small-town busy body and police chief's girlfriend on purpose? Who knows?

"Well, duh!" I roll my eyes. "I should hope so. It's your job to snoop."

"I have your number, Ms. Dukes," Mrs. Bickerson says. "I know all about you."

"You don't even know me!" Renée smacks her chest and looks at Mrs. Bickerson again. "I was trying to help Mysti. Her family was worried about her," she claims. "Are you judging me because of what *she* said?" she spits out the word *she* like it tastes bad and jerks her thumb toward me.

"*She* wants to know why you lied about being in

Mysti's motel room," I interject, using the same tone of voice as Renée.

"I didn't lie to you about that," Renée insists.

"You told me you'd never spoken to Mysti," I clarify. "If that's true, why were you in her motel room?"

"How do you know I was in her motel room?" Renée narrows her eyes and scowls at me with more intensity.

Shoot! How do I talk my way out of this? I can't admit I know Renée's fingerprints were on the forensics report. Eric shows me evidence in confidence. He could get in trouble, and it could compromise the investigation. *Think, Megan, think!*

"I saw you."

Renée and I turn and look at Mrs. Bickerson.

"You saw her?" I clarify. "You saw Renée either enter or leave Mysti's motel room?"

"Both," Mrs. Bickerson replies. "Mysti saw her too. Friday morning. Mysti and I planned to meet at the park. I arrived first. When Mysti got there, she realized she forgot her cell phone. I drove her back to the Hav-a-nap motel to get it. When we got there, we saw Ms. Dukes picking the lock to room 107. I wanted to call the police or the motel office, but Mysti wouldn't let me." She points at Renée. "You were inside for less than five minutes. Then you left."

Mrs. Bickerson opens a desk drawer and pulls out her phone. "Mysti wouldn't let me call anyone, but I took your picture." She extends the phone toward

Renée. "Want to see?" Mrs. Bickerson thrusts the phone toward Renée, but Renée doesn't take it. "You can take my phone, destroy it, and wipe the memory. I have copies in multiple locations online and offline. I'm a librarian, I know where to put stuff."

Busted!

"You and your friend here"—Renée flicks her wrist in my direction—"manipulated those photos with photo editing software."

"Maybe we should let the police decide. Hmm?" Mrs. Bickerson suggests, though it sounds more like a threat than a suggestion. "I gave physical copies of the photos to Mysti when she told me you blackmailed her. I think you killed her when she confronted you with them."

"You blackmailed Mysti?" I look at Renée wide-eyed while I process this latest bombshell.

"Of course not!" Renée retorts. "Mysti approached me when she realized I was tailing her. I admitted her family hired me to locate her. She begged me not to tell them where she was and offered me ten thousand dollars to keep her secret."

"That's not how Mysti told it," Mrs. Bickerson says with a chuckle. "Mysti said you blackmailed her, and I believe her."

"Mysti isn't even her name," Renée hisses.

"I know," Mrs. Bickerson whispers with a wink, then raises her index finger to her lips in a *shhh* motion.

"That entitled brat tried to fleece *me!* Not the other

way around!" Renée stomps her foot. "She counter blackmailed me. She told me she'd report me for breaking into her room if I didn't give her ten grand. I'd lose my PI license with charges for a crime like that!"

Sounds like a motive to me. No wonder Renée didn't look at the photos on Mrs. Bickerson's phone; she knows they exist because she saw them when Mysti showed them to her. Eric hasn't mentioned anything about the police finding photos of Renée breaking into Mysti's motel room.

"Your story keeps changing, Renée," I say in a calm voice. "It's getting hard for a small-town busybody like myself to keep up."

"*Humph!*" With her nose in the air, Renée swings the door open, points her chin in the air, and marches out of the office and down the hall.

"She left within the fifteen-minute time limit." Mrs. Bickerson comes out from behind her desk and closes the office door.

"Was that true?" I ask. "Do you have pictures of Renée coming and going from Mysti's room?"

"Mmm-hmmm." Mrs. Bickerson nods, unlocking her phone. "I'll text them to you."

"Thanks," I say, still shocked by the exchange and disappointed that I allowed myself to sink to Renée's level. "I have to share them with the police."

"I know." Mrs. Bickerson nods. "It's time I talked to them anyway," she adds. "I know Mysti's story. I know who she was. And I know why she ran away from her old life. She told me about her scam and how it works, but despite that, Mysti didn't con me. Her gift was genuine, Megan. The messages she gave me were real. When I tell the police that, they'll dismiss me as a deluded, desperate woman who's wasting their time. They'll discount everything I say. Even the part about Renée Dukes."

"I don't think they'll discount you. I'm sure they'll believe you," I assure her. "Why did Mysti confide in you about her old identity?" I ask.

"She didn't," Mrs. Bickerson explains. "Boris did."

"How did Mr. Bickerson figure out Mysti's true identity?" I ask, interrupting her.

"He's a stock market hobbyist," she explains. "He recognized her from research he did on MD Biocorp stock. They include photos of the majority shareholders and board members in the annual report or something. He showed me her picture on the company website."

If Mr. Bickerson knew how wealthy Mysti was, no wonder he resented the money Mrs. Bickerson paid for readings.

"Mysti admitted it when you confronted her with her photo," I surmise.

"She told me everything." Mrs. Bickerson pulls a new tissue from the bottomless tissue box and dabs her swollen eyes. "It was like a dam had burst, Megan. That poor child was so relieved to have someone to talk to. She was the loneliest soul I've ever met."

Unable to hold it in any longer, my eyes also fill with

tears for the tragic, lonely end of Mysti's life. Mrs. Bickerson slides the tissue box across the desk. Holding hands with Mrs. Bickerson, I use my free hand to take a tissue from the box and dab my eyes, hoping to contain the mascara before it runs down my face.

"Police!" Eric bellows, throwing the door open with one hand while his other hand holds his sidearm. His eyes dart around the room, assessing the situation. "What's going on?" he asks, perplexed by the sombre scene.

He shouts something over his shoulder to the officers in the hallway and holsters his weapon.

I'm crying, Mrs. Bickerson is crying, and we're holding hands over the mountain of tissue between us. Kilian emerges from under the desk to sniff around Eric's feet. I silently hope he doesn't decide to pee on Eric like he did on Adam.

"We're fine," I say with a sniffle. "Why are you here?"

"Hannah called me," he replies.

"Hannah?" I jump to my feet. "Is she OK?"

"She's fine." He puts a hand on my shoulder. "She thought you and Mrs. B were in trouble."

"Why would Hannah think that?" Mrs. Bickerson asks.

"Because her friend Cecily sent her a text saying a woman burst in and was holding you two hostage," Eric says with a chuckle.

I shrug. "We weren't hostages, per se."

"But it was a heated discussion," Mrs. Bickerson interjects.

"It's true?" Eric asks, stunned.

"No, but I can see why Cecily had that impression." Mrs. Bickerson stands up. "I'll be right back. I need to check that everything is OK in the library."

Eric closes the door behind Mrs. Bickerson when she leaves.

"Babe, why are you crying?" He sits in the chair next to me and takes my hand. "What happened?" He uses his thumb to wipe a tear from my eye.

I tell him everything, starting with Renée Dukes's confrontational entrance, and ending with Mrs. Bickerson's revelation that she knew all about Mysti and tried to help her when Renée allegedly blackmailed her.

"Looks like I'll be late tonight," he says with a sigh when I finish.

I nod.

CHAPTER 18

WEDNESDAY, June 16th

April: Think we'll catch anything in the rain?

Me: Mrs. B said rain or shine, so I hope so.

April: See you soon!

When I got home last night, I called April and updated her on everything that happened yesterday. We found ourselves with a sudden, overwhelming urge to visit the fishing pier. We're angling for one fish in particular—a cantankerous, frugal species called Boris.

"Wanna go outside, Soph?" I wrap my fluffy robe around me and tie the belt at my waist.

Sophie leaps off the bed, and when I open the bedroom door, the corgi sprints down the hall. The door to Eric's home office is closed, so I assume either he's in there, or Jax accepted our invitation and is asleep on the pullout sofa.

According to the evidence, Eric slept here last night.

His dirty clothes are in the laundry hamper, and judging by the damp towel on the towel rack, someone used the shower before me.

Yesterday was busy and exhausting. After I brought April up to speed, I had some leftover chicken salad, ran a hot bath, and went to bed early. I was sound asleep when Eric came home.

Sophie catapults into the backyard when I open the door. While she does her business and completes her first perimeter check of the day, I prepare her breakfast and put it on the floor.

Next, I rummage through our collection of coffee pods, searching for inspiration. Hazelnut vanilla sounds like it will hit the spot.

I wipe Sophie's wet paws with a towel we keep by the back door for this purpose. While she eats, I take my coffee upstairs to have a shower.

"Good morning, sleepyhead!" Eric says as I pass his office, the door now open.

That's one mystery solved.

I give him a facetious eye roll for calling me sleepy head. It's barely 6:30 a.m. for crying out loud.

"Hey, handsome," I say, leaning against his desk and putting my mug on his coaster. "I wasn't sure you were in here."

"J stayed at the apartment. He'd already unpacked, so it made sense," Eric explains. "I was on the phone. I didn't want to wake you and Hannah, so I closed the door."

"Who else is up this early?" I ask.

"The cops staking out Renée Dukes's motel room."

"You're watching her?" I ask, wondering what I missed while I slept.

"More like waiting for her," Eric clarifies. "She disappeared after she left the library yesterday. We finally found her late last night when she sauntered into The Embassy. She was already drunk, so I told the officers not to approach her, just tail her. She stayed until last call, then took a cab to the motel. They're still keeping an eye on her. When she surfaces, they'll bring her in for questioning."

"Have you heard the saying, the only honest people are toddlers and drunk people?" I ask. He shakes his head. "Wouldn't it make sense to question Renée when she's drunk? She'd be less inhibited and might be more likely to tell the truth."

"It would be inadmissible," Eric says. "The court would consider her incapacitated."

"Renée and Jax have the same alibi," I say. "If she confirms that she saw him at the park when Mysti was killed, it will eliminate Jax as a suspect, right?"

"I'm not hopeful, babe," Eric confides. "Jax didn't recognize Renée when I showed him her photo. He didn't see her at the park on Sunday morning. We've canvassed like crazy, and we can't find any witnesses who can place Jax or Renée at the park when Mysti was murdered. If she doesn't verify his alibi, it's like neither of them were there."

"We'll just have to find another way to eliminate Jax," I say with more confidence than I feel. "Did you find the pictures of Renée breaking into room 107?" I ask. "The ones Mrs. Bickerson took on Friday morning. I assume Renée took them when she killed Mysti."

"They weren't with Mysti's belongings, and they weren't in Renée's motel room or car when we searched them," Eric replies. "Renée probably destroyed them. She wouldn't want anyone to find them."

"Why did Renée break into Mysti's room?" I ask. "Mrs. B said Renée was only inside for a few minutes. Whatever she was looking for, she found it fast."

"She wasn't looking for anything," Eric reveals. "She was leaving something. We found a GPS tracking device in the lining of Mysti's suitcase. I suspect Renée broke in to plant the device in case Mysti tried to skip town and give Renée the slip."

"That sounds less than legal," I comment, realizing the more I learn about Renée Dukes, the more I dislike her.

"It is," he confirms. "It's one of the many reasons she's avoiding us."

"You look better than yesterday." I run my fingertips along his clean shaven, chiseled jawline. "More like the Eric I'm used to." I comb my fingers through his well-groomed hair.

"I feel better," he says, pulling me onto his lap. "I slept for like six hours." He kisses me good morning.

He smells so good; I missed his woodsy scent. I

wrap my arms around his neck and breathe him in for a moment while he spins us in slow semi-circles in his office chair. He spins us toward the door when we hear the *clickety-clack* of Sophie's nails trotting down the hall.

"Hey, Sophie." Eric rubs her head when she puts her front paws on his chair. "Did you miss me? Wanna go to the dog park?"

Sophie hops onto the sofa across from us and rests her chin on the armrest.

"Were you late because of Mrs. Bickerson's statement?" I ask.

"No," he replies. "Her statement didn't take as long as you'd think, considering how much information she shared," he says, still spinning us in lazy half-circles. "If only her husband was half as cooperative," he mumbles.

"Did Mrs. B know Happy Hour's true identity?" I ask. "I was going to show her the picture of Happy Hour and Mysti, but I didn't get a chance."

"She knew the same as Jax. Mysti met Happy Hour at The Embassy where they got drunk and commiserated about Happy Hour's boyfriend. According to Mrs. B, Mysti *had a feeling* Happy Hour's boyfriend *would get what was coming to him.*"

"Ominous," I comment.

"Anyway, after I questioned Mrs. B, I had to finish questioning Cole Duffy," Eric explains. "I was in the middle of interviewing him when I got Hannah's call that you were in trouble."

"You just left him there?" I ask. "At the station? The entire time?"

"It was unavoidable, babe." He shrugs. "He called a lawyer while I was gone, so the interview was over, anyway."

"I'm sorry you rushed to the library for no reason," I say. "Mrs. Bickerson and I were never in danger. Renée was loud and obnoxious, but she wasn't dangerous."

"I'm just glad I got the call," he says. "I turn my ringer off when I'm in an interview. If anyone other than you or Hannah called, it wouldn't have come through."

"You have Hannah's number on bypass?" I ask, touched.

Bypass means even when Eric turns off his notifications, or mutes his phone, calls and texts from Hannah and me still get through.

"Of course." He winks. "My two most important people."

That comment earns him a kiss.

"Did you learn anything useful before Cole Duffy's lawyer showed up?"

"He denied arguing with Mysti at the Hav-a-nap on Friday. And he denied being on Water Street on Saturday afternoon, despite Lucas positively identifying him as the man he saw following Mysti."

"I'm not surprised," I admit. "He denied it to me too." I sip my coffee. "What else did I miss while I slept?"

"Let's see," he says, looking up at the ceiling. He brings the chair to a halt. "The dress I found in the garbage can is the murder weapon."

"Wow! Good job, honey!" I commend.

"Wanna see the report?" he asks proudly.

"Sure," I say, getting off his lap.

He leans forward and touches his mouse to wake up his laptop. When the screen comes to life, there's a full-screen photo of a baby looking back at us.

"Umm... who's baby?" I ask.

"Isn't he adorable?" Eric gushes. "The pregnant officer at work had her baby last night," he replies. "Another reason I was late."

"How did someone else's baby make you late?"

"She wasn't due for another three weeks. When she went to the hospital, I had to find someone to replace her. She was on desk duty, assigned to the evidence room. She thought she had indigestion. Another officer convinced her to go to the hospital." He points to the screen. "This little guy was born a few hours ago. She emailed his photo to the department. He's cute, eh?" He leans forward and closes the email with the baby's picture.

Does Eric have baby rabies? I've never seen him swoon over a baby before.

I'm worried the brief moment he thought Jax might be his son triggered Eric's biological clock or something. Do men have biological clocks?

"I'll pick up a baby gift," I say.

"We already got them a gift," he reminds me. "Last month, remember? From their baby registry. One of those spinny, musical things that hangs over the crib."

"A mobile," I say. "I remember now."

Eric shows me the forensic report that explains how the fibres in Mysti's lungs and nose match the fibres on the dress he found in the garbage can.

"Oh my gosh!" I declare, noticing the time on his laptop. "I have to get dressed and leave." I grab my coffee from his desk and turn toward the door.

"Isn't it your morning off?" Eric asks, looking disappointed. "I thought Hannah was opening the store today?"

"She is," I confirm. "I'm meeting April," I explain, being purposefully vague.

"I was hoping to have breakfast with the woman I love." He grins, taking my hand and pulling me toward him.

"Well then, I'll leave you alone so you can call her," I tease.

"That's not funny," he says, laughing. "Seriously, babe, we haven't had a meal together since Saturday."

"My errand with April won't take long. Can we have breakfast after?"

"Breakfast at Tiffany's?" he suggests. "9 a.m.? That gives me enough time to take Sophie to the dog park."

"You're going to the dog park in the rain?" I ask.

"It's only misting," he justifies, shrugging.

"Why are you so obsessed with the dog park?"

Smirking like he has a secret, Eric leans back and laces his hands behind his head. "Come with us and find out." It sounds like a dare.

"Not today," I respond. One mystery at a time. First, I'll help Eric solve Mysti's murder, then I'll get to the bottom of his obsession with the dog park. "I'll meet you at Tiffany's."

"Do I want to know what you and April are up to?" Eric asks, narrowing his gaze and tapping his finger on the desk.

"No," I reply, "but I'll tell you if you want me to."

He shakes his head. "Be careful, please."

"Always." I smile.

CHAPTER 19

Occasional drops of rain hit the windshield. I run the wipers once to whisk away the rain that has accumulated since we've been here. While Mother nature alternates between drizzle and light rain without committing to either option, April and I strategize our next step.

"If we just walk along the pier until we find him, it'll be obvious we're looking for him," I say. "And it won't be private. Fishing is a quiet activity, the other anglers will hear everything we say."

"We can't wait for him to come to us. We could be here all day," April counters. "You should've brought Sophie. Walking the dog would've been a perfect excuse."

"She had to go to the dog park," I huff, rolling my eyes.

"Right," April responds with an understanding nod

like she knew Sophie would be at the dog park but forgot.

"What's going on with the dog pa—?" I'm mid-question, when April interrupts me by pointing and nodding toward the far end of the small parking lot.

Mr. Bickerson opens the trunk of his car and his upper half disappears inside, like he's rummaging around for something.

"We should approach him before he finds whatever he's looking for and goes back to the pier," I say unbuckling my seat belt.

"Easiest fishing trip ever." April smiles. "We just have to reel him in, Megnifico." She makes a reeling motion with her hand.

"Ready?" I ask, distracted from my dog park question and eager to get this conversation over with.

She nods, and we exit the car, stepping onto the wet gravel.

Mr. Bickerson is whistling "Dock of The Bay" by Otis Redding. Loudly. He whistles the same handful of bars on repeat, like a scratched record stuck on the same few notes.

April and I close the car doors, looking at Mr. Bickerson for a reaction. Nothing.

"I bet he can't hear us over his whistling," I suggest, joining April on her side of the car.

"What he lacks in variety, he makes up for with volume," she whispers, making me laugh.

We approach his car, and Mr. Bickerson pops his

head out of the trunk when the wet gravel crunching under our rain boots matches the volume of his whistling.

"Hi, Mr. Bickerson." I smile. "Fish biting today?" I ask, hoping it's something you ask someone who's fishing. As a non-fisher, fishing etiquette eludes me.

"My dad swears fish are more likely to bite when it's raining," April adds.

"Nonsense," Mr. Bickerson responds, closing the trunk of his car with one hand and holding a plastic rain poncho with the other. "No doubt started by a fisherman trying to justify fishing in the rain to his carp of a wife."

I giggle at his pun.

"What's so funny?" he demands, his thick moustache twitching.

"Your fish pun," I reply. "It's clever."

"It was unintentional," Mr. Bickerson insists.

"The cleverness or the pun?" April mutters next to me, making me giggle again.

"You ladies here to fish?" he asks, unfurling the poncho. "Fishing for gossip is more like it." He laughs at his own joke as he slides the poncho over his head, then straightens his wide-brimmed boonie hat, adjusting the laces under his chin.

"We aren't here to gossip," I assure him.

I'm already frustrated by his insinuations that all wives are carping nags, and because April and I are women, our only pursuit is gossip. We have many interests aside from gossip. I remind myself that, somewhere deep inside, Mr. Bickerson must have a redeeming quality or two. Otherwise, why is Mrs. Bickerson so committed to him?

"If your boyfriend sent you to ask me about the fortune teller, don't bother," Mr. Bickerson warns. "My lawyer told me not to talk to the police without him present."

"Eric doesn't know I'm here." I hold up my hand like I'm swearing an oath. "And I'm not the police."

"But you'll tell Chief Sloane about our conversation, right?" he asks.

"That depends on what you tell me," I answer.

"Here's what you can tell your police-chief boyfriend," Mr. Bickerson says, wagging his finger at April and I. "That fraudster took advantage of my wife's kind nature to swindle her out of our money. It was only a matter of time." He shakes his head, and his laces sway under his chin. "She fleeced the wrong person and got what was coming to her."

"Were you the wrong person, Mr. B?" April asks, getting straight to the point. "I saw how angry you were with Mysti on Saturday. Remember? I intervened before you did something you'd regret." Mr. Bickerson opens his mouth to speak, but April speaks over him. "I can only imagine how hostile you were when you were alone with her."

Apparently, we're using a good-cop, bad-cop strategy, and April is the bad-cop. Except we aren't cops and we didn't discuss this before we left the car.

"I was never… I never touched that woman!" he retorts, appalled at the notion.

"But you don't deny being alone with her?" I clarify.

"I didn't say that either." He scowls at us. "Stop putting words in my mouth. You don't know what happened!"

"You're right," I agree. "We don't know what happened because you won't tell anyone. We have to piece it together using the snippets of truth we know."

"If you think what we're saying is bad," April interjects, "you should hear the conclusions other people are jumping to." She rolls her eyes dramatically from one side to the other, while raising one corner of her mouth and making a *tsk* noise.

"Like what?" he asks, twitching a bushy eyebrow.

The idea of being fodder for the local rumour mill seems to bother Mr. Bickerson.

I look up at April, confused. Seriously? There are rumours? Why didn't April tell me? April widens her eyes and gives me a knowing nod. Ohhh, she's making it up. There are no rumours—aside from the ones I've already heard. I shake my head and refocus.

"Your poor wife is trying to defend you to the entire town, and you aren't making it easy for her," I add, hoping Mr. Bickerson has some capacity for guilt. "This situation is stressful enough for her without having to defend you too. Have you spoken to your wife since yesterday?"

Mr. Bickerson looks at his feet, digging the toe of his rain boot into the wet gravel.

"We're busy people," he says, without looking up. "Sometimes our schedules don't sync for a few days at a time." He shrugs. "Like all married people."

As someone who hasn't had a meal with the love of my life since Saturday, I can't judge him for that comment.

"Well, she spoke to the police last night," I inform him, "because she wants to put this behind her. Behind both of you. If you didn't kill Mysti, why not cooperate with the police? Tell them why you were in her motel room. Do it for Mrs. Bickerson, to ease her stress."

"How do you know I was in her motel room?" he asks, glaring at me. "Does Shanice know I was in Mysti's room?" Looking toward the dreary sky, he lets out a breath, then looks at me. "It was that maintenance guy, wasn't it?"

"Sorry?" I ask, confused.

This is the first I've heard about a maintenance man.

"The maintenance guy at the Hav-a-nap," Mr. Bickerson clarifies. "I should've known he'd finger me."

"You've lost us, Mr. B," April says. "What maintenance guy?"

"After you interrupted my conversation with the fortune teller on Saturday at the park, I met her at her motel room."

"What time?" I ask.

"I don't know," Mr. Bickerson replies. "After you came along, but before dinner."

After April chased off Mr. Bickerson, Mysti read our tarot cards. Soon after, Lucas said Mysti flagged him down on Water Street. He said he drove her to the motel, cleared the room, then left. Not long after that, Jax left Knitorious and said he went straight to the motel. Where does Mr. Bickerson fit in? Was he the person Mysti believed was following her when she flagged down Lucas?

"Mysti's whereabouts are pretty well documented on Saturday," I say. "She had a pretty tight schedule."

"After I left the park, I drove to the motel," he explains. "I was going to the office to ask which room was Mysti's when I saw a maintenance guy fixing the ice machine. I told him I had a meeting with Mysti to find out my future but forgot her room number. He told me to try room 107."

"Was she there?" I ask.

"No," Mr. Bickerson confirms. "I knocked, but no one answered."

"But you said you were in her room," April reminds him.

"Not yet," he responds, holding up his index finger. Then he looks at me again. "I parked in sight of room 107 and waited."

"How long did you wait?" I ask.

"A while," he replies. "But I had podcasts to listen

to, so I was fine," he explains, as if his ability to amuse himself while he waits is my biggest concern.

"When Mysti showed up, did you ambush her?" April asks.

"She came home in a police car," Mr. Bickerson says, wide-eyed. "I thought maybe she was under arrest, and he brought her to collect her things."

"Did you see the police officer she was with?" I ask, unlocking my phone and finding a picture of Lucas in uniform.

"That new officer. The young one who is always with Hannah," he replies.

"Him?" I show him Lucas's picture.

"That's him," Mr. Bickerson confirms. "He walked Mysti to her room. They talked outside for a few minutes, then she handed him her room key. The officer went inside, alone. She stood in the doorway, looking around, all nervous and jittery. When the officer came out, he handed her the key. She went inside and closed the door, then he left."

"How long was the officer inside Mysti's room?" I ask.

He throws up one shoulder. "Maybe two minutes. Three tops."

I let out a sigh of relief. I believe Lucas's story, but it's still nice to know someone can corroborate it.

"How did you get from your car to inside her room?" April asks.

"After the cop left, I knocked on her door," Mr. Bickerson replies. "She answered." He shrugs.

"And she just let you in?" I ask, dubious that Mysti would welcome the man who aggressively confronted her at the park, then showed up at her door unannounced.

"Not quite," he admits. "She took some persuading."

"How did you persuade her?" I probe.

"I threatened to yell her Christian name at the top of my lungs," he replies. "She opened the door but left the chain lock engaged. I whispered her name, so she knew I wasn't bluffing."

"And she let you in?" I ask.

He nods. "She begged me not to tell anyone who she was. She swore she'd leave town and not take another cent from Shanice."

"Result," I say. "You got what you wanted."

"Almost," Mr. Bickerson says. "I wanted our money back. I told her she had twenty-four hours to give it to me, or I'd contact her family and anyone else who might be interested in her whereabouts and her current occupation. Also, I warned her never to contact my wife again."

"You blackmailed her," I clarify.

"Call it whatever you want," he concedes. "What I did was nothing compared to her lying about her gift to take advantage of innocent people. And I didn't demand a penny more than Shanice gave her. I wasn't looking for a profit. I just wanted our money back."

"Of course," April sighs beside me.

"What?" Mr. Bickerson challenges, crossing his arms and adopting a defensive stance. "If you knew who Mysti was, you wouldn't judge me for wanting my money back."

"I know who Mysti was," I tell him. "I know she was… affluent."

He scoffs. "She had so much money, she made affluent people look poor."

"Did she agree to refund the money Mrs. Bickerson paid her?" I ask, circling the conversation back to the topic at hand.

"She said she needed a day. She said she would give me cash on Sunday, then leave town on Sunday night."

"But Mysti died before she could give you the money," I speculate.

"That's right," he confirms. "One of her other scam victims must have got to her."

"You didn't go back to her room on Sunday to collect?" April asks.

"No, of course not," Mr. Bickerson baulks like he's offended by the suggestion. "I was at home. By myself. Shanice took the car to the library. We only have one car. Do you think I walked all the way from home to the Hav-a-nap motel? It's on the other side of town. I guess you think I killed the fraudster, then walked home again?" He throws his hands in the air and rolls his eyes. "Preposterous!"

Mrs. Bickerson told me she was at the library all day on Sunday, except for a quick outdoor lunch with her friend. In theory, Mr. Bickerson could've picked up the car from the library and returned it without Mrs. Bickerson's knowledge.

"Did Mysti say anything else?" I ask. "Or mention anyone? Did anything about her room or her stuff seem weird to you?"

He blinks at me like I'm asking in a foreign language.

"She said her roommate would be back any minute. She mentioned her roommate twice. And she was jumpy. I assumed it was because I was onto her and knew her true identity. She kept looking through the peephole and peeking through the curtains. And she asked if I saw anyone outside." He gestures vaguely. "Lurking, was how she said it. She asked if I noticed anyone lurking outside her room."

"Did you?" I ask.

He shakes his head. "No. I assumed she wanted me to think she was expecting someone, so I'd leave." He snorts. "Or maybe she wasn't all there, you know?" He twirls his index finger in a circular motion beside his temple, an offensive gesture indicating mental health issues. "She said someone was following her, and she hoped I didn't lead them to her."

"Did she say who?" I ask.

"No," he replies. "But she used feminine pronouns. Like it was a woman. She seemed scared. I believe she was scared, but I'm not sure I believe what she feared was real, if you get my drift." He twirls his finger near his temple again.

"Well, she died less than twenty-four hours later," April states accusingly. She digs her fists into her hips and steps toward Mr. Bickerson. I reach out and touch her elbow, prepared to pull her back if necessary. "Maybe her fears were genuine, after all. Maybe she was running for a reason. Did that *ever* occur to you? Just because she had money doesn't mean she didn't have problems. Maybe if you offered to help her, instead of blackmailing her, Mysti would still be alive."

"This isn't my fault!" Mr. Bickerson shouts, jabbing his chest with his stubby finger. "I never touched that woman. I have no responsibility for her death or the choices she made. My conscience is clear!" He leans toward me, narrowing his gaze and pointing. "Make sure you tell your boyfriend that!"

Sputtering unintelligible words under his breath, Mr. Bickerson turns on his heel and stomps toward the pier, his blue plastic poncho wafting like a cape in the lake breeze.

CHAPTER 20

THE DRIVE to Water Street is quiet except for the intermittent scraping of the wipers across the windshield and an occasional huff from April, followed by words like, "insensitive" and "infuriating."

"I didn't realize you were this upset about Mysti's death," I say as we pull into a parking spot behind Knitorious.

"It's not so much about Mysti as Mr. B," April explains. "He's a bully who only cares about getting his money back."

"Mr. Bickerson is the opposite of his caring wife, that's for sure," I agree.

"He held back information that would be valuable to the case," April vents. "Information that cleared a suspect—Lucas—and he's indifferent to his wife's feelings about everything."

I nod. "On the surface, he's difficult to like," I acknowledge. "But he must have some redeeming qualities. Mrs. Bickerson is a practical, intelligent woman with strong opinions. If she puts up with him, there's a reason."

"Do you believe his story, Megpie?" April asks.

"Maybe?" I shrug, unsure. "The part about Lucas driving Mysti to the motel is consistent with Lucas's version of events."

"Because Mr. B knows Hannah and Lucas are a thing. He had to cover his butt in case Lucas saw him in the parking lot. He had to tell the truth about the part you could verify."

"Good point," I acknowledge. "I don't know if I believe his alibi. Maybe he took the car from the library, killed Mysti, then returned it without Mrs. Bickerson knowing."

"Maybe he was watching Mysti and caught her trying to skip town without giving him the money," April theorizes.

"Mysti told Jax she was leaving Harmony Lake on Sunday, after she collected money someone owed her," I think out loud. "I think whoever she blackmailed didn't want to pay her, but didn't want her to share their secret, either."

"According to Mr. B, he blackmailed Mysti, not the other way around," April reminds me. "Maybe he's not a murderer, just a cranky, miserly man."

I check the time on the console. "I'm meeting Eric for breakfast at Tiffany's. Do you want to join us?"

"No, thanks." April smiles. "T needs me at the bakery so she can pick up some supplies. But I'll walk with you."

"Sounds like a plan," I say, sending a quick text to Hannah to make sure she's awake and on track to open the store. I also let her know that Mr. Bickerson verified Lucas's explanation for his fingerprints in Mysti's motel room.

MOTHER NATURE'S oscillating rain-and-mist routine takes a break for our walk along Water Street. The sidewalk is empty except for the odd bird splashing in a puddle.

Taking full advantage of our rain boots, we walk slowly, scanning the sidewalk for the next puddle, then race to stomp in it first.

"Two to one, Megastar!" April declares, jumping in a puddle with both feet.

"I can't compete with your ultra-long legs!" I tease, envious of her long, sinewy limbs.

We resume our slow amble, scanning the sidewalk for the next puddle.

The sky is dreary and grey, and the air is unseasonably cool yet somehow still humid. I'm preoccupied by my hair. I swear I feel it expanding at an alarming rate as it sucks the humidity from the air. Curly hair problems.

"Mrs. B might have a point about Mysti," April speculates.

"How so?" I ask, gathering my curls into a topknot and securing it with the hair tie I always keep on my wrist.

"Maybe Mysti's gift was genuine," April suggests.

April is the open-minded yin to my skeptical yang. She loves conspiracy theories, supernatural phenomena, and the idea that the paranormal is real.

"She told Jax and Mrs. Bickerson how her scam worked," I remind her.

"I know, but you said Mrs. B believed that despite the scam, Mysti told her things that were real." I open my mouth to object, but April points at me and keeps talking. "You said yourself that Mrs. B is an intelligent, practical woman. She would be hard to fool."

I hate having my own words used against me.

"But Mrs. Bickerson *wanted* to believe," I argue. "She's still grieving the deaths of her parents and had a vested interest in Mysti's comforting messages."

"Mysti's predictions about you were dead on," April counters.

"Pardon the pun," I say, bursting with giggles.

"Oh. Oops. Unfortunate choice of words." April laughs. "Admit it, Megadoodle, she nailed your tarot card reading. She predicted a mysterious young man would bring you a message that would change your life, and she was right!" She nudges my shoulder and races ahead of me to the next puddle. "Jax showed up that same day." She stomps her right foot and droplets splatter her jeans way above her knee. "And she predicted death."

"Three to two!" I shout, pouncing into the next puddle before April sees it. "When Mysti read my cards, Jax was her roommate, remember? He probably told her he came to Harmony Lake to find his biological father. Mysti was in town for almost a week when she met Jax. If she saw Eric around town, it would be easy to make the connection. Chances are, she saw Eric and me together, and based her reading on what Jax confided to her, and what she deduced from watching people. She said the death card wasn't literal death. She said it's a transformation from one state to another or something."

"You became an aunt," she responds, glancing over her shoulder. "That's a transformation." April grabs my hand, and dragging me along behind her, she speed walks past the next store. Then she slows us down and drops my hand, glancing over her shoulder again.

"I think someone is following us," she whispers. "Don't look!" she hisses when I turn my head to look behind us.

I hold up my index finger while I pull my phone out

of my jacket pocket. Employing the same trick I used to take a discreet photo of Cole Duffy, I open the front-facing camera. April plays along, bending her knees and pressing her cheek against mine. We smile, and I pretend to take selfies of us but bring the person two stores behind us into focus and snap a photo.

"You think a mum with a baby is following us?" I whisper, looking at the photo. "She's familiar. Have you seen her before?" I hand April my phone.

"Either she's playing our puddle-jumping game by herself, or she's following us. She speeds up when we speed up, and she slows down when we slow down," April whispers, inspecting the photo. "I've never seen her before."

"Maybe she's keeping a safe distance because two middle-aged women playing in puddles is weird," I suggest, not joking.

"Maybe," April says with hesitation.

"Excuse me!"

We turn toward the unfamiliar woman's voice.

"Woo-hoo!" She waves to us with one hand, the other hand steering the stroller toward us as fast as she can without breaking into a run.

Assuming she's a mum in a hurry, April and I separate, making a path for her and the stroller to charge through. But she doesn't charge through. Instead, she and the stroller come to an abrupt halt in front of us.

"You," she says, glowering at me.

Between Renée Dukes, Mr. Bickerson, and now this lady, I swear I've been scowled at, glared at, and huffed at more this week than the entire rest of my life combined.

"Me?" I ask, pointing at my chest and checking behind me in case she's referring to someone else.

"I know who you are," she says in an angry, threatening tone.

April and I step toward each other, closing the gap between us.

"I don't know who you are—wait!" I take a second to process the spark of recognition that ignites in my brain. A glance at the chubby baby and I know for sure. "Mrs. Duffy? Cole Duffy's wife?"

"He told you about me, then!" It's a declaration, not a question.

"No," I clarify. "He pointed you out at the playground yesterday." I extend my hand. "My name is Mega—"

"I don't care what your name is," she snaps, her eyes full of anger and fear. "I'll just call you home-wrecker since that's what you are!"

"Excuse me?" I demand.

I look around, making sure no neighbours or fellow shop owners are around to witness or hear this.

"You heard me, you… you… FLOOZY!"

Is floozy a popular word again? Does it mean something different now? Is it still a 1910 insult for a woman of questionable morals? It's so hard to keep up with the evolution of language. According to Hannah, *bad* means good, and *sick* means something is amazing.

"Floozy?" April repeats, confused.

Aghast and speechless, my jaw hangs open, and I stare at the woman and baby in front of me, processing her accusation. Mrs. Duffy's furious voice doesn't match her body language. Her grip on the stroller is shaky, and her knuckles are white. Her chin quivers, and she swallows hard, like she's fighting back tears. She has the heavy, exhausted eyes of a mother with young children, and her short, wavy hair is damp, either from the rainy weather or a recent shower. She's a woman in survival mode. I remember the over-whelm of having one baby. I can't imagine it three times over.

Mrs. Duffy adjusts the stroller's rain cover, peeking at her sleeping baby. I'm struck by the realization that she chose the word *floozy* to get her point across, without exposing her son's tiny ears to the much nastier insult she wanted to hurl at me.

"You heard me," Mrs. Duffy says, pointing her chin so it's parallel to the ground. "Don't deny it. I've known about you and Cole for months." Her eyes narrow, and she hisses the word *months*. "I'll kill you before I let you tear apart my family."

"Whoa!" I say. "Let's not say anything we'll regret." By *we*, I mean Mrs. Duffy.

"This woman?" April looks at Mrs. Duffy, but points to me. "This woman right here? You think she's having an affair with your husband?" April laughs, like Mrs. Duffy just told us a joke. "That's absurd."

"It is absurd," I agree. "But. It's. Not. Funny." I say to April through clenched teeth.

April stops laughing.

"Mrs. Duffy, I don't know why you think... what you think.... but you're wrong. I only spoke to your husband once. Yesterday at the playground. Your daughter wanted to pet my dog. Your husband and I made small talk. That's it. I swear."

"You're lying," Mrs. Duffy insists, but the tone of her voice doesn't match her confident words. "You're gaslighting me. Just like Cole does."

Gaslighting is when someone tries to convince you that your perceptions aren't real. The gaslighter says and does things to make their victim question reality and second guess what they know or believe to be true. They challenge their victim's recollection of events until the victim questions their own memories and experiences. Or they trivialize their victim's thoughts and feelings until the victim believes every thought and feeling they have is an unjustified overreaction. Gaslighting is a form of emotional abuse that's difficult to see because it's subtle to the observer and often happens within personal relationships.

"We aren't gaslighting you," April assures Mrs. Duffy, her defenses softened by the woman's obvious distress.

"I believe you, Mrs. Duffy," I say. "If you believe

your husband is having an affair, I do too. But it's not with me."

It's obvious this conversation is too big for the sidewalk in front of Tiffany's. I invite Mrs. Duffy and baby Duffy to join me for a coffee. Reluctant at first, the frazzled mum finally agrees, and I hold the door for her while she maneuvers the stroller inside.

CHAPTER 21

"You can go. I'll be fine," I whisper to April after Mrs. Duffy is inside the diner. "Don't you have to work at Artsy Tartsy today?"

"No way!" April hisses. "She threatened to kill you. I'm not leaving you alone with her, and I'm not hearing about this second hand." She unlocks her phone. "I'll get one of the kids to cover for me." April walks past me into the restaurant.

Tiffany's is an homage to the iconic Audrey Hepburn movie, Breakfast at Tiffany's. The booths, chairs, and stools feature Tiffany-blue pleather uphol-stery and framed images from the movie adorn the walls. Because it's a breakfast restaurant, mornings are their busiest time. Like now. Scanning the sea of heads, I don't spot an empty table or booth.

"A booth just freed up," the cheerful hostess tells us.

"I'll seat you in two minutes." She holds up two fingers. "We just have to clean it first."

"Great," April says. "Thanks."

While we wait for our table, the hostess offers to park Mrs. Duffy's stroller as it's a safety hazard to park it near the table and block the aisle. The baby, now awake, loves this idea and looks over his mother's shoulder with his smiley, drooly face, taking in the new scenery. I offer to take the diaper bag for her while the hostess parks the stroller. Checking the time on my phone, I remember I'm supposed to meet Eric here in ten minutes.

Me: I'm sorry to do this, but can we push back breakfast? Something came up.

Eric: Is everything OK? How long do you need?

Me: Yes. 30 minutes? Or we could do dinner instead?

Eric: I'll see you at 9:30 a.m.

Me: Thank you!

We order three coffees and diffuse the awkwardness by oohing and aahing over baby Duffy, who's bouncing on his mother's lap. He's learning to use his fine motor skills by picking up pieces of dry cereal with his thumb and index finger. He's six months old and not a very good sleeper, though he's a wonderful eater. Teething is hard, and Mrs. Duffy jokes that she has the bags under her eyes and a laundry pile of drool-soaked bibs to prove it.

The server delivers our coffees and disappears. By

instinct, we move the mugs of hot liquid out of the baby's reach before adding our preferred condiments.

While we sip our coffees, and Mrs. Duffy bounces the baby on her knee, pulling various toys and snacks out of the diaper bag to keep him amused, she tells us how she found out about her husband's affair.

"Did you confront him with your proof?" I ask, engrossed by her story of months spent stealthily collecting texts, cell phone records, and credit card statements to prove his infidelity.

"Cole is very persuasive," Mrs. Duffy explains. "He has a way of convincing me it's me. Like I read too much into things or misinterpret everything he does. He has an excuse for everything, and by the time we finish discussing it, he has me convinced he's the victim, and I'm paranoid and suspicious. I end up apologizing to him."

"I'm sorry," I say, wondering if she recognizes Cole's actions as abuse.

"I came to my senses a couple of weeks ago," she says. "The night we arrived at our rental cottage in Harmony Lake. I forgot baby food, can you believe that?" She laughs. "I left it in a cooler bag on our kitchen counter in the city. After we put the kids down for the night, I got in the car to find some."

We pause briefly and discuss the various local options for procuring baby supplies. After two weeks in Harmony Lake, Mrs. Duffy has already discovered most of them.

"Anyway, when I returned to the cottage, Cole was inside on his cell phone. His phone connected to the Bluetooth in our car. He didn't know it happened. I heard their entire conversation."

"Was it the other woman?" April asks, enthralled.

Mrs. Duffy nods. "She's in Harmony Lake." Her chin quivers, and she blinks tears out of her eyes. "They were planning a rendezvous."

April and I gasp.

"Does she live in Harmony Lake, or is she visiting?" I ask.

"I'm not sure," Mrs. Duffy admits. "But this trip makes so much sense now." She shakes her head. "Under the guise of a family vacation, Cole could keep me busy looking after three kids while he had booty calls with his girlfriend," she sneers. "He thinks I don't notice he takes three hours to buy diapers? Or two hours to pick up takeout? Either he's dumber than he looks, or he thinks I am."

"It's him," April and I assure her in stereo.

A familiar, unpleasant stench fills the air, and Mrs. Duffy throws the diaper bag over her shoulder and excuses herself to change the baby.

"Her husband sounds like a total…"

The server comes by with the coffee pot, interrupting April's profane assessment of Cole Duffy, and offers to refill our coffees. We thank her and decline, then she moves to the next booth.

"The man his wife describes is the opposite of the

devoted, proud family man I met at the park yesterday, or in Wilde Flowers," I say, remembering that Phillip told me Cole bought flowers for his wife.

"What if Cole Duffy's mistress was Mysti?" April hisses.

"I don't think so," I whisper. "The Duffys arrived in Harmony Lake on the first of the month. Mysti checked into the Hav-a-nap on the sixth. Mrs. Duffy said the mistress was in town when they got here."

"Maybe Mysti stayed somewhere else first," April suggests.

"You could be right," I agree. "I'll ask Eric where Mysti was on the first."

"If Mysti was Cole's mistress, maybe he killed her because she threatened to tell his wife," April theorizes. "Or maybe she blackmailed him, and he killed her."

"Or maybe Mrs. Duffy killed her," I theorize. "If she mistook me for Cole's mistress after one brief encounter at the park, maybe she also accused Mysti and killed her." It sounds far-fetched when I hear myself say it, but it's not impossible.

"You think Mrs. Duffy killed Mysti, then realized Mysti wasn't the other woman, and continued to hunt for her husband's mistress?" April paraphrases.

"I don't know," I whisper. "But she threatened to kill me on the sidewalk."

"When my kids were babies, I was too tired to kill anyone," April says. "And I only had two kids. She has three. Under age four. Ugh! Just thinking about it makes me want to take a nap."

As Mrs. Duffy weaves through the tables and booths on her way back from the restroom, I tell April I'll be fine if she leaves.

"I've monopolized enough of your day with my drama." I smile.

"Are you kidding?" April says. "I love your drama. It's the only drama I get in my boring life."

"Mrs. Duffy won't try anything in a packed restaurant. Besides, I think she knows I'm not the woman she's looking for."

"Only if you're sure," she says, finishing the last mouthful of coffee in her mug.

When Mrs. Duffy returns to the table, April excuses herself and says goodbye to Mrs. Duffy and the baby.

"Call me," April mouths over her shoulder on her way out, bringing her thumb and pinky finger to her face like a phone.

"I want to apologize for accosting you earlier," Mrs. Duffy says, handing baby Duffy a bottle of something milky. "When I saw you talking with my husband at the park yesterday, and you laughed together, I got the wrong idea." Her mouth smiles, but her eyes don't. It's a sad smile. "I added two plus two and got five. The sleep deprivation on top of everything else doesn't help."

"I understand," I say. "What will you do?"

"I don't know," Mrs. Duffy says with a hopeless

sigh. "I can't continue looking for her, though. It's become an obsession. I suspect every woman I see." She exchanges the baby's damp bib with a fresh one from the bottomless diaper bag. "My parents want me to leave him," she discloses. "My mother is a psychologist, and she says Cole is a narcissist. My father spends his time devising escape plans for me and the kids." She sighs again. "Until today, I would have done anything to save my marriage. But why should I be the only one trying?" She shrugs. "I think I'll call them when I get back to the cottage."

"Listen, Mrs. D—"

"Call me Angela," she interrupts.

"Angela?" I confirm.

I'm sure Phillip said Cole's wife's name was Kelsi with an i. Phillip never forgets a name; details are his thing. If Cole was having an affair with Mysti, who's Kelsi?

"OK, Angela." I smile. "I'm Megan."

Angela Duffy extends her hand, and I shake it.

"Well, Megan, I should get going," Angela says, tossing stuff into the diaper bag. "This one still naps in the mornings, and the other two will be running their father ragged."

"Angela,"—I place a gentle hand on her wrist and lean toward her—"Cole bought flowers yesterday."

"How do you know?" Her eyes narrow into angry slits.

"I was at the florist when he paid for them," I explain. "The florist is my neighbour."

"Cole hasn't bought me flowers since Valentine's Day."

"Pink peonies," I add. "I'm sorry, I thought you should know. I'd want to know."

She nods and, without another word, slings the diaper bag over her shoulder and stands up.

"This isn't the most stroller-friendly establishment," I say, standing up. "I'll help you out."

As we pass the server, I explain that I'm not finished with the booth, and I'll be right back to order breakfast. The restaurant is wall-to-wall people, and Mrs. Duffy decides to settle the baby in the stroller outside.

"Can I ask you one last question?" I ask as we wait for the line of diners waiting to be seated to let us pass.

"Sure," she says, threading through the line with the baby smiling at me over her shoulder.

"Where were you and Cole on Sunday morning?"

"Let's see…" She stops in front of the first set of doors. "Cole was on a three-hour diaper run,"—she snorts—"and the kids and I waded in the lake for crayfish with the family next door."

Angela opens the first set of doors and steps aside while I push the stroller through. She's about to open the second door, but someone outside beats her to it.

"Hey, babe!" Eric beams at me, holding the door open with Angela's hand still on the handle. He looks from me to Angela. "Can I help?" He uses his foot to hold the door open to free up his hands.

Angela looks at me. "You know him?"

I nod. "Eric Sloane, Angela Duffy." I gesture between them. "Angela, this is Eric, our local police chief."

"Let me take that," Eric says, eyeing the stroller and extending his hands.

"Thank you," Angela grunts, thrusting the baby into his waiting arms.

I don't think either of us saw that coming.

Shocked because he expected the stroller, Eric embraces the baby who coos and smiles at him. Eric gushes at the squishy, squirmy bundle of warmth while the baby charms him with gurgly baby noises and drooly, gummy smiles. Baby Duffy giggles with glee when he reaches out to touch Eric's face, and Eric pretends to snap at his chubby, dimpled fingers.

I hand the stroller to Angela. She prepares it for the baby and tucks the diaper bag in the basket underneath, while I watch Eric with the baby. The contrast between this handsome, muscular, strong man, and the tiny, vulnerable baby he holds gently with such tenderness almost makes my ovaries explode. Almost.

"Here you go," Eric says, passing the baby to Angela. "I think you have an appointment at the station this afternoon."

"That's right," Angela confirms, taking the baby and

easing him into the stroller. "At naptime. I should be there around 1 p.m."

"We can come to your cottage if it's easier for you," Eric offers.

"No way," Angela chuckles. "I'm not giving up the chance to go somewhere alone! Even if it is a police interview. Their dad can watch them for a couple of hours."

We say goodbye, and Angela gives me an unexpected side hug, which I return. Then she turns and pushes the stroller up Water Street.

"We're going to talk about Mysti's murder over breakfast, aren't we?" Eric asks, opening the door.

I nod. "You might be late for your one o'clock with Angela," I joke, walking into the restaurant.

CHAPTER 22

WHEN WE RETURN to the booth, the server is wiping the table, laying out paper placemats that double as menus, and cutlery wrapped in tiffany-blue paper napkins. Eric orders a coffee and I order a water, sad because I've maxed out my self-imposed daily two-coffee limit.

"I'll get your drinks and be right back to take your order," the server says with a smile.

We go through the motions of perusing the menu, but it's a formality. We always order the breakfast special.

"So," Eric says, reaching across the table and taking my hand. "What does Angela Duffy have that I don't?" He teases me about postponing our breakfast thirty minutes, so April and I could have coffee with Angela.

"A motive to kill Mysti," I reply, "and an alibi."

Eric arches his eyebrows with interest, but before we

can continue, the server returns. He lets go of my hand and sits back while she places our drinks on the table.

A squealing baby draws my attention to the counter where a man holds a baby over his head. He zooms the baby and makes airplane sounds. Watching the baby squeal with delight, I can't help but flashback to a few minutes ago when Eric was holding Baby Duffy. Holding a baby suits him. He'd be a wonderful father. While I'm certain I don't want more children, raising Hannah was the most satisfying, joyous part of my life. How can I deny him the opportunity to experience that? I know we have to talk about it, but I'm scared. What if I'm right? What if Eric wants kids? It would be irreconcilable. There's no compromise for something this huge. One person would get what they want, and the other would get eternal resentment. Neither of us could live with knowing the other made such a significant sacrifice. We'd have to end our relationship.

"Megan!" Eric squeezes my hand, bringing me back to the here and now. "Welcome back," he chuckles.

"How would you like your eggs?" the server asks me, her pen hovering over her order pad.

"Unfertilized!" I exclaim.

Wrinkles corrugate between her eyes, as the server looks at her pad, unsure what to write.

"Scrambled." Eric smiles at the server, then looks at me. "Right, babe? You meant scrambled?"

"Scrambled," I agree, nodding.

"What was that about?" Eric asks when the server leaves.

"Do you want to have a baby?" I blurt out.

As soon as I say it, I realize it sounds like a suggestion instead of an attempt to open a discussion. Like when someone says, *do you want to go to a movie?* They mean they want to go to a movie and want you to go with them. They aren't trying to start a discussion about the film industry.

"Do you?" he asks with expression that conveys concern, hesitation, fear, and confusion at the same time.

"It came out wrong," I say, squeezing his hand. "I mean,"—I take a deep breath and blow it out—"have recent events caused you to reconsider your position on parenthood?"

Eric squints at me with a confused grin. "You sound like Adam when you talk like that," he says, referring to my lawyer ex-husband. "Where is this coming from?" he asks.

He leans across the table and laces his fingers with mine.

"Your expression when you met Jax," I explain. "You were awestruck when you thought you might have a son."

"It shocked me to see someone I'd never met look so much like my brothers and me," he clarifies.

"Upstairs in the apartment, when Jax told us his birthday, you were disappointed when you realized he wasn't your son. Your whole demeanour got... sadder."

"Relief," Eric insists. "I was trying to hide how relieved I was. I didn't want Jax to feel bad because I was happy he wasn't mine."

What he says makes sense, and he sounds sincere, not like he's trying to protect my feelings.

"You were so disappointed about Jason's reaction to Jax. You talked about how if you were his father, you would have embraced him and made him feel welcome."

"I was disappointed in Jason, babe, not jealous of him. I felt bad for Jax because he felt rejected."

"What about your colleague's baby?" I challenge. "You were gushing over the picture she emailed you."

"When someone on the team has a baby, it's like the department gets a new family member," he explains. "I've watched her belly grow since day one. I was excited and happy for her."

"Thank goodness," I say with a sigh of relief, feeling my shoulders drop about three inches.

"So, you don't want to have a baby?" he asks, dubious. "Right?"

"No," I reply. "Why would you think that?"

"You were so sad Jax wasn't my son. I worried it gave you... ideas."

"I was sad for you, because I thought you were sad," I clarify.

Eric's turn to let out a sigh of relief.

"And the way you stared at the baby picture on my computer this morning," he says, "It's like you were daydreaming." He shrugs. "You were wistful or something."

"I was scared," I admit, "of this conversation." I squeeze his hand and look into his brown eyes. "I don't want kids."

"You do not know how relieved I am." He grins. "The way you looked at me when I was holding Mrs. Duffy's baby…"

"OK, you didn't imagine that one," I admit. "I had a bit of a wobble when I saw you with him." I look into his eyes and will myself not to blink. "A moment of weakness. A very brief moment."

"I like our life. I want to focus on my career without worrying about balancing it with a family," Eric assures me. "Including Jax, I have five nieces and nephews. There's no risk of the Sloane bloodline going extinct. And if I ever feel an absence of children in my life, I hang out with them until it passes." He shrugs with a smile. "And if Hannah has kids, I'll be the most hands-on step-grandfather ever."

The server appears with our food, and we sit back.

"Are we good?" Eric mouths as she places the plates in front of us.

I nod, smiling and relieved.

We thank the server, and she flits to a nearby table where a diner is waving to get her attention.

"Can you tell me about Angela Duffy's motive and

alibi?" he asks, reminding me of all the things I've learned today.

Starting from the selfie I took when April and I were puddle-jumping and ending with the moment Angela and I bumped into him at the door, I tell Eric about our impromptu coffee date with Angela and her baby.

"Incredible," Eric says, shaking his head. "You're the only person I know who can turn a hostile confrontation into a friendly coffee klatch. She accused you of having an affair with her husband, called you a floozy, and threatened to kill you. Half an hour later, she's hugging you goodbye after trusting you with her deepest, darkest secrets. Extracting information is your superpower." He sips his coffee. "I should hire you to work for the HLPD."

His flattering assessment makes me blush.

"Some of her behaviour can be attributed to sleep deprivation." Full, I push my plate of half-finished food toward him.

"Sleep deprivation isn't an excuse for threatening to kill you, babe." He jabs my sausages with his fork and transfers them to his plate. "Neither is accusing you of having an affair with her husband based on a quick glimpse at the park. It sounds like Mrs. Duffy isn't thinking rationally."

"And it sounds like Cole plays head games with her. You know, gaslighting her and manipulating her. I get the sense it's making her not think straight."

I'm struck by how ridiculous I sound, defending a

woman who threatened to kill me and called me a floozy.

"So, let's say Cole and Mysti were having an affair," Eric muses. "Then who is Kelsi?"

"Another mistress?" I venture a guess. "I'm certain Phillip said the flowers were for Kelsi with an i. You know Phillip. He's very particular about details. He never forgets a name."

"Cole has a wife and at least two mistresses?" Eric pushes his plate aside and pulls out his notebook and pen.

"I don't know," I reply. "I'm just trying to come up with scenarios that fit the evidence."

He grins at me, his eyes full of pride.

"Did Cole leave Wilde Flowers with the pink peonies?" he asks.

"No," I shake my head, thinking back to yesterday. "Just him and the baby."

"So, Phillip must have delivered them," Eric surmises. "I'll assign an officer to contact Phillip and get the address. Whoever Kelsi is, we need to talk to her. And if Cole kills his mistresses, we have to do a wellness check on her."

"You and April don't know anyone local named Kelsi?" he asks.

I shake my head. "Neither of us knows anyone named Kelsi, period. Local or otherwise."

"I'll get to work verifying Cole's three-hour trip to

buy diapers on Sunday," he comments, making notes in his notebook.

"Angela said she caught Cole speaking to his mistress—whoever she is—on the first of the month. Where was Mysti on the first?" I ask.

"Our first confirmed sighting of Mysti in Harmony Lake is on the sixth," Eric says. "I've pieced together most of her movements for the three months before her death, but there are gaps. I suspect the gaps were when she travelled between towns. She probably stayed in motels that accepted cash and laid low until she needed to make more money. The first of the month fell into a gap."

"You would've found Cole's number on Mysti's phone if they were seeing each other, right?" I ask.

"Mysti rarely used her phone," Eric reminds me. "It's a burner. For all we know, she replaced it every week." He shrugs. "We're still waiting for call records from the landline in her motel room, and the pay phone in the parking lot of the motel."

"Huh! Payphones," I say. "I thought they were obsolete. I didn't realize the Hav-a-nap still has one."

"The Hav-a-nap has one," Eric responds. "There's one at The Embassy, one near the town hall, and a couple by the waterfront."

Now that he says it, I realize he's right. It's surreal that I pass these payphones every day without being consciously aware of them.

"Mysti could've used any of those," I realize out loud. "She was in all those places."

Eric nods.

We pause our conversation while the server clears our dishes and refills Eric's coffee.

"By the way," he says, pouring cream into his mug, "Mysti's family is issuing a press release about her death today." He stirs his coffee. "Dinnertime, I think." He pulls out his phone and swipes a few times, then hands it to me across the table. "Want to read it?"

I take the phone and read the press release the family's lawyer emailed to Eric. It says, "Everley Leighton Moregard-Davenhill, 29, of Toronto, Ontario, Canada died unexpectedly while vacationing at an undisclosed location. The Moregard-Davenhill family has no further comment, as Everley's death is part of an active investigation by local authorities. The family requests that the media respect their privacy during this difficult time."

"Vacationing? She was in hiding," I comment, passing Eric's phone back to him. "At least they didn't mention Harmony Lake by name or the date she died. It'll be difficult for the media to connect Everley Moregard-Davenhill to Mysti Cally."

"Doesn't matter," he says, shaking his head. "It's not hard to find a suspicious death matching her age and description and figure it out. Lucky for us, Mysti was rich and could have vacationed anywhere on the planet. They have a large search area, but the media will figure it out and show up here sooner or later."

"Got it." I nod, acknowledging his warning.

"What else did you and April do this morning?" He sips his coffee.

"Nothing," I reply, playing coy. "We fancied an early morning walk at the pier, that's all."

"In the rain?"

"It's only misting." I mimic Eric's tone of voice and shrug when he said these exact words about taking Sophie to the dog park in the rain this morning.

Shaking his head, Eric tries but cannot suppress a laugh. "Smart aleck," he mumbles between snickers. "Let me guess..." He pretends to think hard. "The fishing pier by chance?"

"As a matter of fact…"

His phone chimes, interrupting us.

"Hmph!" he says, reading the screen. "Guess who's at the station offering to give a statement?" I shake my head, having no clue who it could be. "Boris Bickerson," Eric replies, his thumbs typing a response.

"Wow!" I say, shocked and pleased.

I guess Mr. Bickerson has a conscience, after all.

"Does his sudden cooperation have anything to do with you and April?" he asks.

"I doubt it," I say with a chuckle. "He was *not* happy to see us this morning. If anyone convinced him to talk to the police, my money's on Mrs. Bickerson."

We pay for breakfast, and Eric walks me to Knitorious because that's where he parked. We take our time, taking advantage of a break in the rain, and I tell him about my and April's conversation with Mr. Bickerson. I put particular emphasis on the part where Mr. Bickerson's version of events corroborates Lucas's version of events, verifying that my daughter's boyfriend told the truth about how and why his fingerprints ended up all over Mysti's motel room.

Eric stops walking just before we reach Knitorious and pulls my hand, turning me toward him.

"Please don't tell Hannah, yet." His serious expression tells me now isn't the time to tell him she already knows. "Tell her after Mr. Bickerson signs his statement. In case he changes his story. It might prove Lucas told the truth about driving Mysti to the motel and checking her room on Saturday, but it doesn't prove Lucas wasn't in her room on Sunday morning. He still has no alibi for Mysti's murder."

"I'll manage Hannah's expectations," I assure him.

I wish I could make this go away for her. Hannah's too young to worry about her boyfriend being implicated in a murder. We need to solve Mysti's murder so my daughter can get on with her life, murder-free like someone her age should, and my boyfriend can get on with his life, getting to know his newfound nephew as a person instead of a person of interest.

CHAPTER 23

"IT'S WEIRD, RIGHT?" I ask Jax when Sophie drops the orange tennis ball at my feet, after I threw the blue rubber ring for her. "She ignored the blue rubber ring on purpose and brought back a ball instead. What other dog does that?"

"Isn't Sophie trained to only bring you tennis balls?" Jax asks like it's a generally accepted fact.

"What?" I ask. "Where did you hear that?"

"I just assumed," he stammers, shifting his weight uncomfortably. "I'm sure Sophie's normal." He rushes to the other side of the deck with his face focussed on his phone.

I'm the only person in Sophie's life who's worried that her bizarre new habit of fetching and retrieving anything except the toy I throw is a symptom of something serious. Can two-and-a-half-year-old dogs get dementia? Is it possible she forgets which toy she's supposed to bring back? I don't think Sophie has vision problems; she doesn't bump into things. Do corgis go through a rebellious phase? Is she trying to express her individuality?

"Mum, Eric's home," Hannah announces, closing the screen door behind her and dropping into a lounge chair with a heavy sigh. "He said he'll join us after he changes out of his work clothes."

"OK." I pick up the squeaky rubber squirrel and lob it across the yard. "Start the barbecue in about ten minutes," I instruct as I watch Sophie ignore the rubber squirrel and sniff around it. "I'm going inside to start the potatoes and make the salad."

Sophie happens upon an old, weathered green tennis ball, picks it up, and prances proudly toward the deck. I throw my hands in the air, frustrated. I give up.

The sun forced its way through the clouds about an hour ago. The air is still cooler than it should be for mid-June, but it's barbecue weather, nonetheless. When you live somewhere that gets snowfall warnings seven months of the year, you learn to broaden your definition of barbecue weather.

"Hey, handsome," I say, when Eric joins me in the kitchen.

He presses his hands on the counter on either side of me, caging me between him and the counter, and kisses me hello.

"Is Hannah all right?" he asks, looking through the

window behind me. "She looks like she lost her best friend."

"Something like that," I respond, ducking under his arm to free myself from his man-made cage. "Today was Lucas's day off. He was supposed to come for dinner. But they changed Lucas's shift because someone he works with had a baby last night. His day off is tomorrow instead of today, and Hannah is stuck with us tonight."

"I don't schedule the shifts," he says, raising his hands to his chest in a don't-shoot-me gesture. "Unless it's an emergency like last night when we needed cover for the evidence room."

"I'm calling the vet tomorrow," I tell him as I slide a tray of mini potatoes into the preheated oven. "I'm worried about Sophie's fetch issues."

"Sophie's fine." He laughs. "There's nothing wrong with her, trust me." He smirks. "She had her annual check-up last month."

No one believes me. Am I paranoid, or does everyone know something I don't?

"What are we having?" Eric asks, rubbing his washboard stomach.

"Spiducci, rosemary roasted potatoes, and Greek Salad," I reply. "Hungry?"

"Always," he replies, looking out the window at Hannah and Jax in the backyard. "I don't want them to overhear," he explains. "Mr. Bickerson gave us a signed statement."

"Yay!" I say. "Did his statement match what he told April and me?"

Eric nods. "You can tell Hannah we verified Lucas's claims about when and why he went to Mysti's motel room on Saturday."

"Excellent," I say, nodding.

"You already told her." It's a statement, not a question.

"Yes," I admit. "But I told her *before* you asked me not to," I explain, hoping to make it seem less sneaky.

"I figured," he says with a sigh. "I questioned Renée today," he informs me. "Oh! and I found out where Phillip delivered the flowers Cole bought."

"You've had a productive day!" My interest piqued, I stop dicing the tomato, put the knife down, and turn to face Eric, giving him my full attention.

"Phillip delivered the flowers to the Harbourview condominium complex," Eric discloses. "My officer knocked on the door to the unit, but no one answered. The doorman said when Phillip delivered the flowers, he called up to the condo and offered to accept them on Kelsi's behalf, but she told him to buzz Phillip up and instructed him to leave the flowers outside the door of her unit."

"So, Phillip didn't *see* Kelsi," I conclude.

"Didn't see her and didn't hear her," Eric confirms.

"The doorman said the unit Phillip delivered the flowers to is a vacation rental. It's not owner occupied. He confirmed a woman has been staying there, but his description was vague. According to him, she comes and goes from the underground parking garage, so he's only seen her twice. The camera footage from the garage is grainy, and the car associated with the condo unit has dark, tinted windows. We ran the plate, and the car is a rental. I'm waiting for the rental company to return my call. They might demand a warrant before they tell me anything."

"Who owns the rental condo?" I ask. "The owner must know who rented it."

"The doorman provided the owner's contact information. I'm waiting for him to call me back," Eric replies. "If Cole's mistress is staying in the unit, I expect he rented the unit for her, but if I'm lucky, he used her name so his wife wouldn't find out. Her last name and contact information should be on the rental application."

"Hi, Eric," Jax says as he opens the back door. "Hannah sent me to get the meat."

"Hi, J," Eric says. "I'll grab the skewers and bring them out in a minute."

"Can you ask Hannah to set the table please?" I ask Jax.

Jax nods and smiles, then returns to the back deck.

"Later?" I ask, referring to the interviews he conducted today.

"Later," Eric agrees, kissing my forehead.

He retrieves the lamb and chicken spiducci from the fridge and goes outside. I continue chopping and dicing vegetables, wondering if the new information Eric gathered today will get him any closer to arresting Mysti's killer.

While we eat, Hannah and Jax devise a plan to meet up with some of her friends for a movie in Harmony Hills. Their plan brings Hannah out of her pining-for-Lucas slump, and Jax is excited to meet people his own age. Jax informs us he has a second interview with the Harmony Lake Fire Department tomorrow, and the three of us assure him a second interview is a good sign.

"If they don't like you, they wouldn't want to see you again," Hannah reasons.

Eric and I offer to clear the table and clean the kitchen, so they won't be late for the movie.

"Drive safe," I remind Jax as he and Hannah put their shoes on. "You're carrying precious cargo."

"My driver's abstract is spotless," Jax states with such seriousness, I half expect him to produce a copy from his pocket and show it to me.

"I'm kidding," I assure him. "I'm sure you're an excellent driver."

"I'm not kidding," Eric interjects, bellowing from the kitchen. "Drive safe."

"He's kidding too," I say to Jax, his expression more fearful than amused. "It's his sense of humour. You'll get used to it."

"Jax can't tell when you're joking," I chide Eric when Hannah and Jax leave. "He's not used to your brand of sarcasm. He's freaked out enough with being a murder suspect, waiting for the DNA results, and the job interviews. Don't stress him out."

"He's fine, babe." Eric grins. "I check in with him every day to make sure he's coping."

"You're a good uncle," I say. "He's lucky he found you."

"He's lucky he found *us*," Eric corrects me, stepping away from the sink and wiping his hands on a dish towel. "It's for the best he didn't find Jason first," Eric confides. "Jason still hasn't warmed up to the idea. He hasn't asked even once how Jax is coping. When I call or text him and mention Jax, he changes the subject and says he has to go."

"Maybe the DNA results will help him," I suggest. "When will we get them?"

"Friday at the latest, according to the link the Let Me Take A Cellfie website sent to Jason and Jax," Eric replies.

At least one mystery will be solved soon.

CHAPTER 24

"ARE YOU WORKING TONIGHT?" I ask.

"I have to answer a few emails, but that's it," Eric replies, shrugging. "I need a night off."

"Yes, you do," I agree. We pour another glass of wine and move to the family room. Anticipating the move, Sophie's already situated on the sofa, curled up for her after-dinner nap. "You didn't correct me about Jax being stressed because he's a murder suspect. I assume if Renée placed him at the park when Mysti died, you would have told him you eliminated him."

"Your assumption is correct," he says. "No one can place Jax at the park. He may as well have no alibi."

"None of the suspects have an alibi," I say, looking for a silver lining.

I reach for the coffee table and pick up the lap blanket I'm assembling and the next square in the pile.

"Yup. We have five suspects and zero verified

alibis." Eric sips his wine and puts the glass on the table, which Sophie interprets as an invitation, so she crawls onto his lap, and he automatically strokes her. "Jax, Renée, Lucas, Cole, and Mr. Bickerson." He raises a finger for each name.

"The blackmail note you found in Mysti's throat implies her killer is someone she blackmailed," I remind him. "The only suspect Mysti blackmailed was Renée Dukes."

"That doesn't mean Mysti didn't blackmail someone else," Eric points out. "It just means we don't have evidence of another blackmail scheme."

"Let's try to get into Mysti's head," I suggest, placing the lap blanket and crochet hook in my lap. "Why would she blackmail Jax?" I ask. "He just graduated from school and doesn't have the ten thousand dollars she demanded. Also, he's barely twenty-two years old. How many secrets can he have that would warrant extortion?"

"You're right about his financial situation," Eric reveals. "I looked at his bank records, and Jax couldn't have paid Mysti that much money. But his inability to pay the blackmail demand gives him a motive to kill her."

"What information could she have about him?"

Eric shrugs and picks up his wine glass. "Everyone has secrets, babe." He takes a sip.

Though they knew each other for less than forty-eight hours, Jax and Mysti shared a lot of information with each other. At least, she shared a lot of information with him—how her scam worked, that she was running away from her family, that someone was stalking her. Maybe the information Mysti shared with Jax was part of a strategy to get Jax to share information with her. Jax said Mysti knew what questions to ask to get information. Maybe exchanging secrets was one of her strategies. Jax is young, naïve, and trusting. I could see him confiding in her if he believed she was a friend.

"What about Mr. Bickerson?" I ask. "He has no alibi and refused to talk to the police until today. Also, Adam overheard him threaten to kill Mysti."

"Adam overheard Mr. Bickerson threaten to kill *someone*," Eric clarifies. "Mr. Bickerson didn't use Mysti's name. I'm sure he meant Mysti, but I can't prove it. He admits he was in Mysti's room, and he admits he blackmailed her for the money Mrs. Bickerson spent on Mysti's… services."

"He knew Mysti's real name before anyone else in town. He knew she was rich. Do you believe he settled for blackmailing her only for the money Mrs. Bickerson paid her, or do you think he wanted more?"

"I don't know," Eric says. "The story he told you and April is consistent with the statement he gave me today. We did a thorough background check on the Bickersons and didn't find any skeletons in their closet. If Mysti blackmailed Mr. Bickerson, she did it with information we can't find."

"I think the prime suspect is Renée," I assert. "And

I'm not saying that because I don't like her. She outright lied about talking to Mysti and about contacting Mysti's family. And she broke the law when she broke into Mysti's motel room and planted the GPS tracker. Also, she admits that Mysti blackmailed her for ten thousand dollars, the same amount written on the note you found in Mysti's throat."

"I agree it doesn't look good for Renée Dukes." Eric nods. "But unless I can place her at the scene of Mysti's murder, the evidence is circumstantial. And the other suspects create reasonable doubt. A murder charge wouldn't stick."

"There has to be a way to prove it." I think out loud. "Can you at least charge her with breaking into Mysti's motel room and planting the GPS tracker?"

"She could face charges for those things and blackmail," Eric replies. "She admitted she blackmailed Mysti and Mysti counter-blackmailed her. Renée's hoping if she cooperates with us, we'll reduce or eliminate any charges against her.

"Did you show Renée the picture of Mysti and Happy Hour?"

"Renée didn't recognize her," Eric replies. "The picture was taken on the ninth. Renée didn't arrive in Harmony Lake until the tenth. She wasn't tailing Mysti yet." He sighs. "But I'd really like to find this Happy Hour person and ask her some questions. I can't help but feel like she's the missing link who can help piece this puzzle together."

"I'll put Happy Hour on project status tomorrow," I offer. "If she stayed in Harmony Lake, and hung out at our local pub, someone local must have noticed her and had an interaction with her. She's not invisible."

"While you're searching for invisible people, Cole Duffy's mistress is another person I need to talk to," Eric continues. "Cole's lawyer provided a receipt for the diapers he purchased on Sunday morning, but a single purchase at the pharmacy ten minutes away from their rental cottage doesn't explain his two-and-a-half-hour absence or prevent him from killing Mysti. He admits he had a mistress but won't tell us who."

"Had a mistress?" I ask. "Past tense? Like, he had a mistress, but she died?"

"Your guess is as good as mine," Eric replies. "I'm trying to get a warrant for his cell phone records. Until then, we only have circumstantial evidence. Lucas saw Cole on the sidewalk when Mysti flagged him down on Saturday. But that doesn't mean Cole was pursuing her. His presence could've been a coincidence. Jax saw him arguing with Mysti outside her motel room on Friday, but Cole claims he was warning Mysti to leave his wife alone."

"Did Angela Duffy verify Mysti harassed her on the beach like Cole claimed?" I ask.

Eric nods. "Mrs. Duffy said Mysti approached her at the beach and offered her a free tarot card reading. Mrs. Duffy said Cole shooed Mysti away before she could take her up on it."

"Angela Duffy wanted the reading?" I clarify. "According to Cole, Angela said no. He said he intervened because Mysti wouldn't take no for an answer."

"According to Angela, she didn't say yes or no because Cole answered for her."

"Why would Mysti offer Angela a free reading?" I ask. "Free readings don't pay the motel bill."

"The free reading could be a ploy," Eric theorizes. "Maybe Mysti used a free reading to get people hooked, then charged for subsequent readings."

"Like free samples at the grocery store." I nod.

"Prior to Harmony Lake, Cole Duffy and Mysti never crossed paths," Eric reveals. "If Mysti was Cole's mistress, their relationship started in Harmony Lake, and it evolved fast."

"What about Lucas?" I ask. "I think he's the least probable suspect. Mysti only met him once. What kind of secret could she uncover in one brief interaction? And it would be dangerous to blackmail a cop, knowing other police departments wanted to question her. Mysti was too smart to take that risk."

"She only met him once *that we know about*," Eric corrects me. "Just because there's no evidence to support it, doesn't mean it didn't happen," he explains. "It could just mean I haven't found the evidence yet."

My face flushes with heat, and not from the wine. "Do you think Lucas was seeing Mysti?" My tone is accusatory and defensive at the same time. "And I don't mean so she could predict his future."

"No," Eric replies, rubbing the back of my neck. "I think Lucas Butler is a trustworthy guy, otherwise I wouldn't have hired him. But my personal opinion is irrelevant. My personal opinion doesn't solve murder cases, evidence does."

"How do you prove a negative?" I demand. "How do you prove something didn't happen?"

"By proving what did happen."

We're talking in circles. I'm unable to ignore my emotional attachment to the outcome, and Eric has a frustrating ability to switch off his emotions and ignore anything that isn't evidence; I call it cop mode.

I huff and sip my wine, incensed at the idea of someone betraying my daughter's trust.

"Babe, I want to eliminate Lucas as a suspect too. At least as much as Jax. But I can't let my feelings steer the investigation. Even a hint of personal bias could affect the investigation and compromise the case. It could help the killer avoid consequences."

"I know." I nod. "I understand what you're saying, I just don't like it."

Eric pulls me into him and wraps his arms around me. Something digs into my hip. I reach between me and the sofa cushion and yank out Sophie's rubber squirrel. She must've snuck it into the house when we came inside for dinner. I toss it down the hall. Sophie vaults off the sofa in pursuit of the thing. I rest my head in the crook of Eric's neck where it meets his shoulder, and he kisses the top of my head. I relax there for a moment, letting his rhythmic breathing soothe me.

"We're going to solve this case," he whispers. "We're close. I can feel it. I always get a feeling right before a case breaks open."

"You're more confident than me," I say, sitting up and finishing my wine. Sophie drops a yellow tennis ball at my feet. I want to ask her where the rubber squirrel is but say nothing.

"I have an amazing partner," he says with a wink. "We haven't met a killer yet we couldn't catch."

Is he trying to convince himself or me?

CHAPTER 25

THURSDAY, June 17th

"Good morning, ladies," I greet Mrs. Roblin and Mrs. Vogel.

I opened the store ten minutes ago, and they're already here, settling in for a day of knitting. Sophie gets out of their way, leaping off the sofa and climbing into the sunny display window for her early morning nap, which differs from her late morning nap on her dog bed.

"Good morning, Megan!" the ladies say, almost in unison.

"Did we miss Eric?" Mrs. Roblin asks, pointing at my iced vanilla latte on the counter.

Her voice is full of disappointment.

"I'm afraid so," I confirm. "He visited before the store opened. He's busy today, so I doubt we'll see him until dinnertime."

"Oh, that's a shame," Mrs. Vogel adds. "I made date squares for him." She pulls a Tupperware container out of her knitting bag. "There's extra for young Jax too." Then she pulls out an insulated lunch bag. "In case your hobby requires us to stay over the lunch hour," she explains with a grin.

"Why don't I put them in the fridge," I offer, jerking my head toward the back room.

"Are you sure?" Mrs. Vogel asks.

"We wouldn't want to impose," Mrs. Roblin asks, producing her lunch bag from inside her knitting bag.

"It's not an imposition," I say. "I'll put them away for you. You don't have to sit here all day. I appreciate it, but I'm sure you're bored with being here by now."

"Nonsense," Mrs. Vogel says. "We love it here."

"It's so much more exciting here than the library or coffee shop where we usually knit," Mrs. Roblin says.

"Good morning," Hannah smiles at us.

"Where did you disappear to?" I ask.

"Upstairs," she replies. "Jax asked me to help him choose from a bunch of ties Eric lent him for his second interview today. He doesn't want to wear the same tie twice."

"Second interview?" Mrs. Vogel asks, her eyes narrow. "With the Harmony Lake FD?"

"That's right," I reply.

"The fire chief hasn't decided yet?" Mrs. Roblin asks, as if she expected him to decide by now.

"I guess not," I reply. "Pardon?" I ask, sure Mrs. Vogel said something.

"Nothing, dear," Mrs. Vogel smiles, unlocking her phone and tapping away on the screen.

I'm sure Mrs. Vogel mumbled something that sounded like *I'm on it*, under her breath. Then Mrs. Roblin nodded, giving Mrs. Vogel a conspiratorial sideways glance.

I smile, collect their lunch bags and date squares, and head to the kitchenette.

This forces me to give the fridge an overdue clear-out. I open the compost bin and put it on the counter next to the fridge, then pull the garbage bin over so it's next to me. I empty the fridge, wash and disinfect the shelves, then ruthlessly toss old food, rearranging the remaining contents.

"Good Morning, Aunt Megan," Jax says behind me.

"Good morning," I say, spinning around to greet him.

"I hope it's OK to call you Aunt Megan?"

"Of course, it is!" I insist. "I like the sound of it! Congratulations, by the way," I add, hoping congratulations is an appropriate response to DNA results. "Your uncle told me the email was in your inbox when you woke up this morning."

"Do you know how to tie a tie?" he asks, holding up Eric's two-tone pink necktie.

"Isn't your interview this afternoon?" I ask, looping

the tie around his neck and adjusting the length of the ends.

"Yes," Jax confirms, "but I want to get everything ready. My dad showed me how to tie a tie, then Uncle Eric showed me how to tie a tie. He tied it for me before my first interview. I just had to tighten it. Now, I can't remember how to do it."

"We've got you covered," I say, flipping one end of the tie over the other. "This is one of my favourite ties. Eric hasn't worn it in ages since he dresses business casual most of the time now." I pull one end through a loop and make a few adjustments. "There." I tighten it but leave enough slack so Jax can get it over his head. "Did he lend you the matching pocket square, too?" I ask.

Jax nods. "Yes. Thank you," he says, inspecting the Windsor knot in the mirror by the back door. "Maybe I'll find a how-to video online and practice with another tie."

The pink tones in the tie around Jax's neck remind me of the blush-pink dress Mysti wore in the selfie with Happy Hour, which reminds me I promised to put Happy Hour's identity on project status today.

I unlock my phone and find the selfie of Mysti and Happy Hour. I copy the photo and edit the copy, cropping Mysti out of it. Then I send the photo of just Happy Hour to Hannah.

Me: Can you ask around and see if any of your friends recognize her?

Hannah: OK. Is she related to Mysti's murder? Followed by a scared face emoji.

Me: Possibly.

When I return to the store, Hannah is binding off another blanket square. This is the third day this week Hannah has knitted. In just three days, Mrs. Roblin and Mrs. Vogel have achieved something I've never been able to accomplish. They've turned my daughter into a knitter. I even noticed yarn and needles in her room when I walked past her bedroom last night.

THE FOUR OF us knit in comfortable silence—well, the three of them knit, I'm crocheting the last lap blanket with the square Hannah just finished. Hannah pulls out the yarn and needles I saw in her room. She's working on a scarf with a handwritten pattern Mrs. Roblin gave her.

"Don't tell him, Mum!" Hannah demands. "It's a surprise for Christmas. I'm making Lucas a scarf, hat, and mitts. Mrs. Roblin is helping me. They're her patterns," she says.

"He won't hear it from me," I promise.

"Good morning, Mayor Martel," Mrs. Vogel says when the door opens.

"Hello, ladies," Adam says to the all-female craft contingent. "How is everyone today?"

"What brings you to Knitorious today?" I ask, after everyone exchanges pleasantries and some light gossip.

"The postal carrier delivered your mail to Latte Da by accident." Adam drops the envelopes on the counter. "I offered to drop it off on my way to the town hall. Also, I thought I'd congratulate Jax on the email he got last night. If he's around," Adam says, not mentioning the DNA results.

"He's upstairs getting ready for a job interview," Hannah explains.

"If you hurry, you might catch him," Mrs. Roblin adds. "We're all pleased about his test results." She smiles.

How does Mrs. Roblin know about Jax's DNA test results?

"Will there be a party to give him a proper welcome?" Mrs. Vogel asks.

"We'll do something," I reply, "when Connie gets back from Europe."

"I texted him, Dad," Hannah says. "Jax says you can go upstairs if you want."

"Thanks, Princess," Adam replies.

I look at Adam and smile. "I have some mail for a few stores between here and the town hall."

"And you'd like me to drop it off on my way?" he surmises.

"Thank you, Adam! That would be great," I respond as if he offered.

Adam follows me to the harvest table, where I pick up three stacks of mail and hand them to him.

"The new postal carrier is getting better," I say, as he reads the addresses on the envelopes. "This is only the second day this week she's mixed up the mail. If she doesn't mix it up tomorrow, it'll be her best week yet."

"How do the charity knitters already know about Jax's DNA results?" Adam whispers as I walk with him toward the apartment stairs in the backroom. "I thought he just found out a few hours ago. Eric only posted it in the Modern Family group chat a few minutes ago."

The Modern family group chat is our group text thread for all the members of our non-traditional family of choice.

"I assume Hannah told them," I whisper, shrugging. "Otherwise, their influence extends beyond the borders of Harmony Lake and all the way to the Let Me Take A Cellfie labs."

"I know you're joking," Adam says with a chuckle. "But it's a scary possibility."

Adam disappears into the backroom, his feet thudding on the stairs up to the apartment.

He's right. With their extensive network of informants in every nook and cranny of this town, the charity knitters might know who Happy Hour is. And if they don't, they can probably find out faster than me.

I open the cropped photo of Happy Hour and walk over to the cozy sitting area.

"Ladies, do either of you recognize this woman?" I hand my phone to Mrs. Roblin.

She pats the top of her head, then her chest, then looks around, finally locating her reading glasses on her lap. She puts them on and examines the photo.

"I don't recognize her," Mrs. Roblin says, shaking her head. She hands the phone to Mrs. Vogel.

"Me neither," Mrs. Vogel says. "Is this related to your hobby?"

"Could be," I say. "I'm not sure. Eric needs to find her."

"Would you like us to help?" Mrs. Roblin asks.

"If it's not too much trouble," I say, smiling.

"No trouble," Mrs. Vogel insists. "Text me the photo."

"We told you we're here to help, Megan," Mrs. Roblin reminds me with a smile.

Mrs. Vogel hands the phone back to me and I text Happy Hour's photo to her. As I hit send, Adam returns from the upstairs apartment and announces he's leaving.

"Can you drop these at the library?" I drop my phone on the counter and grab the bag containing the last of the lap blankets. "Mrs. Bickerson is expecting them. The library is in the same building as the town hall," I reason, thrusting the bag toward him.

"Technically, the library is next door to the town hall," Adam corrects me. "But fine. I'll take them. What kind of mayor would I be if I refused to deliver lap blankets that will benefit sick and isolated residents?"

"Thank you," I say, smiling.

"Why do you have a picture of Kelsi on your phone?" Adam says, nodding at the photo of Happy Hour on my phone.

Kelsi? Are Happy Hour and Kelsi the same person?

"Kelsi?" I ask, making sure I didn't mishear him. "You know her?"

"Not well, but we've met. She's renting a condo in my complex. Our underground parking spots are near each other.

"Do you know her boyfriend?" I ask.

"No, but I know she wasn't happy with him last week."

"I'm listening," I say, encouraging him to continue.

"I was getting in my car to pick up my dinner order at The Embassy, and Kelsi was getting out of her car in the underground garage. She was yelling at her boyfriend on the phone."

"Did you get his name by chance?" I ask, interrupting.

"She called him several names," Adam replies. "But none of them were proper names, if you catch my drift."

"What were they fighting about?" Hannah asks, joining us at the counter.

"It sounded like he either cancelled plans with her at the last minute, or he stood her up. I'm not sure which.

But it wasn't the first time, and Kelsi was fed up. She told him she never wanted to see him again. She had to yell extra loud because the reception down there is awful."

"How did you find out her name?" I ask.

"After she hung up on her boyfriend, she asked me if I was familiar with Harmony Lake. I told her I'm more familiar than most people because I'm the mayor. I introduced myself. She introduced herself."

"Did she tell you her last name?" I probe.

"No," Adam replies. "She introduced herself as Kelsi. This is her first time visiting Harmony Lake. She and her boyfriend were supposed to spend time together working on their relationship, but he was messing her around."

"Why did she ask if you were familiar with Harmony Lake?" Hannah asks.

"She wanted to know where she could *drink her cares away*, as she put it."

"Did you recommend a place?"

"The Embassy," Adam confirms. "It was happy hour that night. I told her if she hurried, she could enjoy half price drinks for two hours. I gave her directions, then just offered to drive her, since I was going there, anyway."

"You drove her to the pub?" I confirm.

"Yup. We walked in together. She thanked me for the lift, and I gave her a card for the Precious Cargo Cab company so she could get a cab home."

"Did you have a drink with her?" I ask.

"No, I went straight to the bar to pick up my fish and chips. I didn't pay attention to where Kelsi went."

"Did you see her talking to anyone when you left?" I ask. "Did she meet anyone?"

"Not that I saw," Adam recalls. "But I left right after I got my order."

"Eric might call you," I say. "Thanks for dropping off the mail and the blankets."

Adam says goodbye and leaves, weighed down with mis-delivered mail and lap blankets.

I'm taking a moment to process the information Adam just gave me when my phone rings and vibrates in my hand. Eric's name and picture flash on the screen.

"I'll be right back," I say as I walk toward the backroom.

"Hello?" I say, closing the door behind me.

"Hey, babe. You won't believe this. The owner of the rental condo got back to me. I was right, the condo was rented in Kelsi's name. Anyway, he gave me her last name and address, and I pulled her driver's license photo from the database." He pauses, then chuckles. "You'll never believe who Kelsi is."

"Happy Hour?"

"How did you know?" Eric asks, dumbfounded that I know and disappointed I ruined his surprise.

"Adam told me."

"Adam? How does he know?"

I tell him about Adam's encounter with Kelsi in the

underground garage, and how it was his suggestion that Kelsi go to The Embassy for happy hour the night she met Mysti.

"I left a voicemail message for Kelsi, and I've contacted the police department in her hometown. They'll knock on her door and contact me if they locate her."

"Locate her?" I ask. "Isn't she staying at the condo?"

"She left last night," Eric informs me. "Took her belongings and left the key with the doorman."

"Oh my," I say. "Do you think she and Cole skipped town together?"

"I'm not sure," Eric admits. "Every officer in town is looking for Kelsi, Cole, and Angela. We can't locate any of them, and none of them are answering my calls and texts. I told you I had a feeling this case was about to break wide open," he reminds me. "Listen, babe. Stay safe. These people are unstable. They might feel desperate, like they have nothing to lose."

"I understand," I assure him. "You be careful too. Keep me up to date."

"I love you."

"I love you too."

I paste a smile on my face, return to the cozy sitting area, and pick up the sock I was working on before lap-blanket assembly took over my life.

"Everything OK, Megan?" Mrs. Vogel asks.

"Yes," I reply. "Nothing to worry about."

Except for the rhythmic clicking of our needles, we

knit in silence, my mind cluttered with flashbacks to all the interactions I've had with people since Mysti died, including with the killer themself. How could I look someone in the eye and talk to them without seeing the evil lurking inside them?

"It's him!" Mrs. Vogel hisses when the bell above the door jingles and Lucas enters the store.

I toss a throw pillow onto Hannah's lap to hide her knitting, and Mrs. Roblin gathers the throw pillow, with the knitting concealed underneath it, and plops it into her large knitting bag.

Hannah jumps to her feet, grinning from ear to ear.

"I promised I'd take Sophie to the dog park," she announces. "Lucas is coming with me since it's his day off."

"Sophie already had a walk this morning," I remind her. "And she'll have another one at lunchtime."

"I promised," Hannah argues with a shrug.

"Why?" I ask. "Why does Eric insist that Sophie go to the dog park every single day?" Hannah and Lucas look at each other, then at me, and shrug. "A simple question no one will answer," I huff.

"So, can I take her?" Hannah asks.

"You know what?" It's a redundant question. Fed up with the dog park, I plonk my knitting on the coffee table. "I'll take Sophie to the dog park!"

I stand up and whistle for Sophie, who leaps off her dog bed and stands at attention. When I march toward the backroom, she trots behind me.

"Ready, Soph?" I ask, attaching her leash and digging my sunglasses out of my bag. "Let's go. I can't wait to see why the dog park is so amazing."

I'm sure dogs are oblivious to sarcasm, but it makes me feel better to vent. I grab Sophie's rubber boomerang toy from the basket by the back door, and we leave.

CHAPTER 26

OUR LOCAL DOG park is actually two dog parks, separated by a dense thicket of trees known as the woods. One dog park is for large dogs, and the other is for small dogs. Sophie hangs out in the small-dog park. It's slow today, despite the picture-perfect June weather. Aside from Sophie, there are only two miniature schnauzers. Sophie recognizes her friends, and as soon as I detach her leash, rushes over to them. The three dogs form a butt-sniffing circle, following each other and saying hi.

"It's amazing they don't get dizzy, isn't it?" The man on the next bench chuckles, looking up from his eReader.

"Yes, it is," I agree. "You must be Salt and Pepper's dad," I say. "I'm Sophie's mum."

"Right," the man acknowledges. "Isn't it funny how, at the dog park, we cease to have our own names and are content to be known as extensions of our dogs?"

"You're right," I say. "It's the same with kids. For years, half the town knew me as Hannah's mum."

"I haven't seen you here in a while," the man says. "Sophie's dad usually brings her."

"He's working," I explain.

Salt and Pepper's dad and I exchange pleasantries and make small talk while our dogs romp and frolic in the open field. When an alarm chimes on his watch, Salt and Pepper's dad puts two fingers in his mouth and summons the twin schnauzers with a loud, shrill whistle. All three dogs respond, loping toward us.

"Hi, Salt. Hi, Pepper," I say to the dogs, petting them when they approach the bench and check me out with their noses.

Their dad attaches their leashes, tucks his eReader under his arm, and we wish each other a good day.

Sophie watches her friends leave until they're out of sight. She looks sad there's no one left to play with.

"Look, Soph!" I wave the rubber boomerang in front of her, to distract her from staring at the space in the distance where she last saw her friends. "Wanna fetch? Get the toy? Wanna get it?" I ask, shaking the boomerang and waving it around.

Once Sophie locks her gaze on the toy, I raise it above my head and behind me, then heave the thing as hard as I can across the field.

"Shoot!" I exclaim, watching the toy veer left, hurl

across the field and into the woods dividing the two dog parks.

I'm not known for my killer throwing arm, so I'm surprised the thing went as far as it did. Around sixty feet is my usual maximum distance, so this is a new personal best.

I hold my breath when Sophie disappears into the woods and I lose sight of her.

"Where are you, Soph?" I mutter, worried a large dog on the other side of the trees caught her attention and lured her away.

I walk toward the woods and whistle for Sophie. Nothing. "Sophie!" I shout. Nothing. I'm about to break into a run when her head, followed by her short, long body, emerges from the underbrush.

"Phew," I sigh, then I whistle and pat my knees.

Sophie charges toward me at full throttle. She over-shoots her target and circles around me before coming to a halt at my feet. She sits at attention and drops a stick at my feet, her ears perked up with pride.

I sigh. "Where's the toy, Soph?"

She looks at me, then at the stick, baffled by my lack of enthusiasm for her stellar fetching and retrieving skills.

"Did you lose the boomerang?" I ask. "Let's find it."

Sophie accompanies me as far as the edge of the open field, then sits while I venture alone into the buggy, brambly woods. It's dark in here, and a dense carpet of evergreen needles, moss, and other foliage makes the boomerang toy hard to find. I open the flash-light on my phone and use it to light my way.

"This isn't worth it," I mumble, scanning the ground for the boomerang. "Sophie has dozens of other toys." I sweep the ground with my foot as I walk, in case the toy is under something. "The boomerang isn't even one of her favourites." A sudden ripple of unease shoots up my spine, causing me to shudder and break out in goosebumps. I stop and hold my breath. Silence. I glance around, making sure I'm alone. I am. Why do I feel like I'm not? "Forget it. I'll order another one online," I convince myself, eager to get back to the open field of the dog park.

I'm about to turn around when I spot the boomerang under a nearby tree.

"Ha! Found it!" I mutter to myself with smug satis-faction.

Bending down to collect the toy, twigs crack behind me.

"Sophie?" Nothing.

If it were Sophie, she would have rushed to me when I said her name. I tell myself it's just a squirrel or a bird. Making as little noise as possible, I retrace my steps toward the dog park. Near the entrance, off the crude path, a man's hat catches my eye. I didn't notice it on my way into the woods. A black baseball-style cap with the words *Dad in charge*, in white font. It's identical to Cole Duffy's hat. Why would Cole be here? Do the Duffys have a dog? *Stop panicking, Megan!* There are probably a million hats just like it. Chances are this isn't even his hat. I should tell Eric anyway, just in case. I unlock my phone and snap a pic of the hat.

Me: Found this at the dog park. I attach the photo of the hat.

Eric: You're at the dog park? In the woods?

Me: Yes. Should I pick up the hat?

Eric: No. Don't touch it. Who's with you?

Me: Sophie.

I walk past the hat toward the opening in the trees that leads back to the small-dog park. When I emerge from the woods, Cole Duffy is standing in front of me. Sophie sits next to him.

Eric: Calling you.

"Good girl, Soph!" I say to the obedient corgi, sitting patiently and wagging her tail. "Come." She trots over to me and sits by my side.

Cole is within arm's reach of me, too close for my comfort, but if I take even one step backwards, he'll be able to push me into the woods where no one will see me. And he's too close for me to run past him and get away.

My phone trills when Eric calls. Cole snatches the phone from my hand. Sophie barks and growls.

"Give it back," I say, extending my hand for the phone.

"You first," Cole responds. "Give me back my wife."

"I don't have your wife," I hiss. Cole turns and

pitches my phone into the distance. "Why would I have your wife?"

Sophie takes off, chasing after the phone, thinking Cole is playing fetch with her.

"You might not have her," Cole admits, "but you know where she is. You convinced her to take the kids and leave me."

"Angela left you?" I ask. "I'm proud of her, but I assure you, I had nothing to do with it."

"Yes, you did. She left me after she met with you for coffee yesterday. You told her to do it. You turned her against me. Just like that meddling fortune teller turned Kelsi against me."

"I did no such thing," I defend myself. "Angela and I talked for thirty minutes, and she did most of the talking. We haven't talked since. Did you follow me here?"

"I was hoping you'd lead me to my wife."

"You dropped your hat in the woods," I say, jerking my head toward the trees. "If you do anything to me, the police will know. I took a picture of the hat."

"Of course, you did." He rolls his eyes.

"What do you mean the fortune teller turned Kelsi against you?" I ask. "Is Kelsi your mistress?" Sophie returns, trotting proudly toward us with a stick in her mouth. She stops in front of me and drops the stick at my feet. "Good girl, Soph," I mutter.

"*Was*," Cole corrects me. "Kelsi *was* my girlfriend. Mistress makes it sound wrong."

"Infidelity is wrong," I remind him, "in most circumstances."

"I love Kelsi. But we met at the wrong time. I couldn't leave my wife, but I couldn't leave Kelsi either. Do you know how hard it is to be in love with two people?"

"I don't," I answer truthfully. "But by lying to them, you took away their right to choose. Maybe Kelsi didn't want to be the other woman. And maybe Angela didn't want to be a betrayed wife."

"Duh!" he says. "That's why I didn't tell them about each other. I knew they'd both leave me, and I'd end up alone."

"Mysti told Kelsi you're married," I assume.

"They met at a local bar right after Kelsi and I had a huge argument. Kelsi told her about me and showed her a picture of us. Mysti had seen me and Angela around town and told Kelsi I have a wife and three kids."

"Kelsi left you?" I ask.

"Yup. At first," Cole admits. "But I convinced her that Angela and I were having a family vacation together for the sake of the kids. I told Kelsi the marriage was over, but Angela and I put up a united front for the kids. She wanted to believe me, but she realized I'd lied to her from the beginning. Yesterday, she stopped taking my calls. She wouldn't answer the door at the condo. I even bought her flowers. Pink peonies, her favourite. She left town last night. It's all Mysti's fault."

"It's Mysti's fault you were unfaithful and lied about it?" I ask. "Is that why you killed her? Because she ruined your... arrangement with Kelsi?"

"It wasn't enough for Mysti to ruin my relationship with Kelsi. She wanted to profit from it too."

Something agitates Sophie. Her ears twitch and something behind me in the woods gets her attention. Not wanting her to spook Cole into doing anything rash or drastic, I hold up the boomerang toy and hurl it in the direction Cole threw my phone. My arm is weaker than Cole's, so the boomerang doesn't go as far as my phone.

"Did Mysti blackmail you?" I ask. Cole looks at me with hesitation. If Mysti blackmailed him, he doesn't want to admit it. "Listen," I say, leaning toward him against my better judgement. "You aren't alone if Mysti blackmailed you. She blackmailed lots of people. Multiple police departments wanted to question her."

"Then I did the world a favour, didn't I?" Cole smirks.

Is this enough to constitute a confession?

"How did Mysti do it?" I ask. "Did she call you? Visit your rental cottage? How did she demand money from you?"

I watch Sophie run past the boomerang. She gets smaller in the distance until she stops and sniffs around.

"She slipped me a note on the beach one day," Cole admits.

"The same day she offered Angela a free tarot card reading?" I assume.

He nods. Mysti's offer of a free tarot card reading to Angela was likely to show Cole she was serious about the blackmail threat.

"I followed her back to her motel and confronted her with the note she gave me," he admits. "She told me she knew all about my relationship with Kelsi. She knew dates and times and everything. If I didn't give her ten thousand dollars in cash by Sunday, she would tell Angela. She rambled off a bunch of gibberish about karma and how I brought this on myself."

This must be the confrontation Jax interrupted between Mysti and Cole.

"Instead of paying her, you killed her?" I deduce.

"Pretty much," Cole admits. "I knocked on her motel room door on Sunday morning and told her I had the money. She told me to leave it and walk away. I told her it was on the ground outside and stepped aside so she couldn't see me from the peephole. When she opened the door, I pushed her into the motel room."

"How did you do it?" I ask.

"Let's just say she choked on her own words." He chuckles at his dark reference to shoving Mysti's handwritten blackmail note down her throat.

"You choked her?" I ask, feigning ignorance about Mysti's cause of death.

"She wouldn't stop screaming after I pushed her inside the room. I had to shut her up. I grabbed the back of her head and shoved her face into the bed. She still wouldn't stop screaming, I pushed harder to muffle the sound. She kept struggling. She was so hysterical that she couldn't hear me telling her to calm down. She kept kicking and screaming, so I pushed her head into the bed harder and harder until she stopped screaming. She stopped screaming and kicking at the same time. I let go and waited a few minutes, but she didn't wake up."

"Why didn't you call for help?" Squinting behind my sunglasses, I see Sophie in the distance, trotting toward us with something in her mouth.

"What would I say? Hello? 9-1-1? Can you send help? The girl I was smothering died." His voice oozes with sarcasm. "I panicked. I wanted to get out of there. I looked around the room for something to use to open the door. Her tarot cards were sitting on the nightstand and the death card was on top. It seemed fitting, so I crumpled it up and shoved it down her throat, along with the blackmail note she gave me."

Boom! The card and note are holdbacks. This is proof that Cole was there when Mysti died.

"Why?" I ask.

"Like I said," Cole replies with a shrug. "It seemed fitting that she should choke on her own words. When I lifted her head to shove the card and note in her mouth, there was a pink dress on the bed. Her face was pressed against it. I wrapped the dress around my hand when I opened and closed the door." He holds up his hands and wiggles his fingers. "No fingerprints, no proof." He laughs.

"Where's the dress now?" I ask.

"Tossed in a garbage bin," he says, waving away his response like it doesn't matter.

But it matters. The pink dress is the second hold-back. Cole just implicated himself in Mysti's murder. If only someone else was around to hear it. Sigh.

Sophie circles us, prancing and showing off her retrieval skills with a victory lap. She stops between us and drops my cell phone on the ground between Cole and I. It rings. Eric's name and picture flash on the screen. He's persistent, I'll give him that.

"You won't need this where you're going," Cole says, bending over to retrieve my phone.

As he bends, I lift my knee with all the strength and speed I can muster.

A sharp *crack* rings out when my knee makes contact with Cole's face.

Was the crack his face or my knee?

Cole brings his hands to his face and drops to his knees in the long grass.

Pain shoots through my leg as I lunge sideways, out of Cole's reach.

"Come, Soph!" I shout. "Run!"

I bolt toward the safety and visibility of the open field. Sophie, being faster than me, is way ahead.

Behind me, I hear Cole yell after me, calling me an

impolite name that rhymes with witch. I don't dare turn around. Trees and bushes rustle behind me. Is Cole escaping into the woods? No, he's chasing me, the thud of his fast footsteps grows louder and I run as fast as I can. I'm tempted to turn around to check, but convince myself to look ahead and keep going. I need a phone. I need to call the police before Cole gets me.

"Megan!"

Cole? How did he catch up to me so fast? I will myself to keep running and not turn around. I have to find help. Of all the days for the dog park to be dead! Pardon the pun.

"Megan! Stop!"

Arms encircle my waist. He's tackling me. I brace myself to hit the ground, but he hoists me into the air. With my feet dangling, I kick and flail. Screaming, I struggle to unclench his hands from my waist while trying to head butt his face with the back of my head.

"It's me," Eric breathes in my ear, bringing us to an abrupt stop.

He sounds like Eric, he smells like Eric, and he feels like Eric, but when he lowers me to the ground, I spin around to check, fearful Cole is trying to trick me.

"Where did you come from?" I ask, breathless.

"PEI originally," Eric quips, winded. I don't laugh. "I was hiding in the bushes. A bunch of us were," Eric explains in response to my underwhelming reaction to his witty comeback. "I was sure Sophie saw me at one point," Eric says, panting. "I thought she would give us away, but you distracted her with the boomerang. Well done." His upper body heaves between breaths. "I was up the street from the dog park when you texted me the hat photo," he explains between heavy breaths. "I drove to the big-dog park and ran through the woods, hoping to sneak up on Cole. I had every officer on duty meet me here. They approached without sirens and turned their radios and phones off so Cole wouldn't hear us." He puts his hands on his knees and catches his breath. "You're faster than I expected. How can someone who hates running be so fast?"

"I guess I hate dying more than I hate running," I justify. "How much did you hear?"

"Enough," he exhales, standing up. "You did great, babe. Are you OK?" With his hands on my shoulders, he looks me over. "I was right behind you. If Cole Duffy tried anything, I would've killed him."

"I'm fine," I assure him, looking around to make sure no one heard him threaten Cole. "Are you OK?" I scan him from head to toe. "Did you get him?"

Eric stands aside, and in the distance, several uniformed officers surround Cole Duffy. He's on the ground, on his stomach, with his hands secured behind his back. His face is smeared with blood.

"I think you broke his nose," Eric says. "That crack when you kneed him was so loud, we all cringed in the bushes."

"I hope he's not too badly injured," I comment. "Will you have to charge me with assault?"

"Of course not. You did nothing wrong," Eric assures me. "The only charges I'm handing out today are to Cole Duffy. You did what was necessary to escape from a psychotic killer."

Too bad Mysti couldn't escape from him.

CHAPTER 27

Sᴜɴᴅᴀʏ, July 4th

"Any luck?" Eric asks when, in a huff, I drop my phone next to me on the sofa.

"No," I say, exasperated. "Jason and his wife go back to PEI tomorrow. This is our last chance to have a family dinner before they leave. Jax and Jason are having an early dinner, then Jax's going to bed early because he starts his new job tomorrow. Connie says she still has jet lag after returning from her trip, and Hannah is helping Lucas unpack before he starts a week of night shifts tomorrow."

The Harmony Lake Fire Department offered Jax a job, and he accepted. He's staying in Harmony Lake, close to his Uncle Eric. Uncle Eric is thrilled.

After he received the DNA results, Jason came to terms with having another son. He and his wife arrived in town two weeks ago. Jason and Jax have spent time getting to know each other.

Eric's brother and his wife are staying in our spare room because our new tenants moved into the apartment above the store. Jax and Lucas. We offered Jax the apartment when he accepted the job with the HLFD, and he asked if he could find a roommate to share the rent. Lucas was still looking for an apartment in town, so it worked out perfectly. Lucas moved in a few days ago, and Hannah has devoted her free time to helping him get settled.

I pick up my phone when it dings.

April: Sorry, Megapixel, T and I have plans tonight!

"April," I inform Eric as I type a response.

Me: No worries!

"They're busy too?" he assumes. I nod. "It's fine," Eric says. "Jax said he doesn't want any fuss."

"I know," I respond. "I just want him to feel welcome and let him know we're happy he's here."

"How was brunch this morning?" Eric asks, changing the subject.

"Poor Lucas was so nervous, I thought he might throw up," I reply. "But Adam was on his best behaviour and even joked around to help Lucas relax. Hannah is happy that her dad is giving Lucas a chance."

"Let's go for a walk, then have dinner at The Embassy," Eric suggests. "Sheamus allows dogs on the patio now, so Sophie can come with us. We'll walk at the far end of the lake."

"The secluded part that the tourists don't know about?" I ask, tempted.

"That's the one," Eric replies.

"Or we could just go to the dog park," I counter. "It would be easier."

"Are you sure?" He looks hesitant, like he doesn't think it's a good idea. "I thought we'd avoid the dog park for a while. At least until your knee heals."

"My knee has healed." I lift the hem of my dress and show Eric my knee. "See? The bruise is almost gone, and it doesn't hurt at all."

I poke at the yellowish mass to prove it doesn't hurt. It hurts a little.

"I don't want you to rush it," he says. "Let's go to the lake instead. We can go to the dog park next time."

"Fine." I shrug. "But the patio might be full in this weather. We might not get a table."

"We'll get a table." Eric smirks.

"How do you know?"

"Trust me." He winks.

"If you say so," I concede and lift myself up off the sofa. "Let's go. It's not like we have a family dinner to get ready for."

"Now?" he asks, sounding unprepared.

"When were you thinking?"

"It's fine." He waves away my question. "We'll go now." He unlocks his phone and starts typing.

"Are you working? On a Sunday?" I ask, suspicious he's not telling me something.

"Loose ends," he replies without looking up from his phone.

"I thought Renée Dukes was the last loose end, and you tied that up days ago."

After the police arrested Cole Duffy for murdering Mysti, Renée ceased cooperating with the police. Mysti's family hired a team of lawyers to represent her. Using their extensive wealth and considerable influence, they made Renée's legal problems disappear. Renée has been incommunicado ever since. Eric suspects Renée accepted a large sum of money from the Moregard-Davenhill family for her signature on a nondisclosure agreement forbidding her from talking about her involvement with the family, or with Mysti. We never found out if Mysti's fear that her family wanted to harm her was legitimate, or an overreaction to a family argument.

"Other loose ends," he mutters, still typing.

"What other loose ends?" I ask, trying to recall what is unresolved.

The police in Kelsi's hometown tracked her down the day of Cole's arrest. Cole didn't harm her. She had no clue he had killed Mysti, or that Mysti used the information Kelsi confided in her to blackmail Cole. Aside from some trust issues, she's fine.

When Angela told me over coffee that she might phone her parents, she meant it. She reached out that day and asked them to help her leave Cole. They were more than willing and arranged a rental car for their daughter. At naptime, Angela went to the police station to give a statement and answer questions. Then, she went back to the rental cottage and gave Cole a short grocery list. She knew he wouldn't return for at least a couple of hours because he'd use the opportunity to visit Kelsi. When he left, she packed their stuff and took a cab to pick up the rental car. She's staying with her parents while she figures out what will be best for her and her children going forward.

"Ready?" Eric asks, shoving his phone in his pocket.

"Ready," I say. "C'mon, Soph!"

Sophie jumps off the living room sofa and meets us at the door.

"Hang on," Eric says. "I'll grab her frisbee."

"SOPHIE WANTS you to throw the frisbee," Eric says when she drops the toy at my feet.

We're sitting on a cluster of large rocks on the shoreline. The sun is hot, and the warm lake breeze creates a vortex of curls around my face.

This end of the lake is less popular with tourists than the rest of the lake because most tourists don't know it's here. Also, it's far from the amenities of Water Street and downtown Harmony Lake, and the rocky landscape is difficult to traverse and leaves very little beach to enjoy.

"Nope," I say, shaking my head. "I don't like this game. If I throw it, she'll ignore it and bring back something else. Then I'll have to search for the frisbee and fetch it myself."

"If Sophie doesn't bring back the frisbee, I will," Eric says, tucking a few curls behind my ear. "Please just throw the frisbee." He kisses me.

"Fine." I pick up the frisbee and wave it around, getting Sophie excited for the impending pursuit. "What's this, Soph? See the frisbee? Wanna chase it? Ready?" I bring the frisbee to my chest and flick my wrist, sending it flying along the shoreline.

In hot pursuit, Sophie follows the frisbee to its landing place, between two rocks, then sniffs around the rocks, her head and upper body disappearing then reappearing between them.

"Here she comes," Eric says, watching Sophie navigate through the rocks with her prize clenched in her mouth.

"I bet it's a stick," I say, venturing a guess at what Sophie will leave at my feet. "Or maybe a shell."

Sophie prances back to us, sits proudly at my feet, and drops a purple tennis ball.

"Good girl, Soph," Eric praises the corgi and rubs her head.

"How did you find a tennis ball way out here?" I

ask, picking up and examining the ball. It's engraved. I hold it up to inspect the gold embossed letters.

"Eric & Megan," I read the top line out loud.

"Now & forever," I read the second line out loud.

Before I can process the weird coincidence that Sophie found a random tennis ball with our names engraved on it, Eric stands up, steps off the rock and takes the tennis ball from me.

Bending one knee, he kneels and opens the tennis ball. The Velcro makes a *sc-tch-tch-ch* noise as the top half of the tennis ball peels away from the bottom. It flips open like a jewellery box and inside the ball, a purple velvet lining cushions an engagement ring.

I gasp and bring my hands to my mouth.

Trembling and with a shaky voice, Eric recites a romantic, corny, sentimental speech he prepared, bringing tears to my eyes.

"Megan Elizabeth Monroe Martel, will you marry me?"

"Yes." I jump to my feet.

Eric stands up, and I launch myself into his arms, wrapping my legs around his waist.

"Look this way and smile!"

Eric pivots us toward Hannah, who is holding up her phone. Where did she come from?

"Are you filming this, Hannah Banana?"

"Live streaming," she replies. "So everyone at The Embassy can watch."

"I'm taking still photos," April says, from behind me.

I turn my head, and April is standing a few rocks above us, her digital camera blocking her face. Cue the ugly tears.

"You planned this?" I ask Eric, straightening my legs so he can lower me to the ground.

He nods. "With a lot of help," he replies, using his thumb to wipe a tear from my cheek. "You're a hard person to surprise. Everyone is waiting for us on the patio at The Embassy."

"Everyone?" I ask. "Is this why they were busy tonight?"

"Yes," he replies with a chuckle.

"And there's nothing wrong with Sophie?" I confirm. "You trained her to only bring me a tennis ball, no matter what I throw?"

"I'll try to un-train her so you can stop fetching her toys."

We laugh.

"Can I see the ring?" Hannah asks. She tells everyone at the Embassy that we're on our way and ends the live stream.

"Eric didn't show it to you already?" I ask, wondering how involved Hannah and April were in his plan.

"No, he said it was a surprise," Hannah replies.

"I haven't seen it either," April shouts, climbing down to our level. "Eric said we couldn't see it until he gave it to you." Eric climbs up and takes April's arm, helping her down to ground level.

After we *ooh* and *ahh* over the ring and Eric's good taste, he suggests we should head over to The Embassy.

"Let's go," I agree, then remember the frisbee. "We should find the frisbee."

"We'll find the frisbee," April offers. "You two go ahead with Sophie. Hannah and I will find the frisbee and meet you there."

"I can't believe you planned all this behind my back," I say once we're in the car.

"Everyone was in on it," he admits.

Hannah helped train Sophie by taking her to the dog park on the days Eric couldn't, to reinforce her new trick of only retrieving tennis balls. Eric booked the patio at The Embassy, and April invited everyone. Connie arranged the menu and ordered the food. Today, April had to contact everyone again to tell them to arrive at The Embassy early because I decided we should walk Sophie right away instead of later, like Eric planned. This was the flurry of texts Eric sent before we left the house, the *loose ends* he was dealing with.

Hannah arrived at the lake before us and hid the ring. Then she hid in the rocks until it was time to livestream the proposal. They chose the spot ahead of time, which is why he talked me out of going to the dog park. We stopped to sit on that rock on purpose, so when I threw the frisbee, it would land close enough to the ring for Sophie to find the purple tennis ball.

"You're stuck with me now," Eric says. "No refunds, no exchanges. Partners in crime forever."

"But maybe with a little less crime."

I unlock my phone and open the text messaging app.

"I'm sure our engagement will be murder-free," he muses. "Who are you texting?"

"My sister," I reply holding my hand in front of me and taking a photo of the ring.

I crop the photo to eliminate the car interior in the background and hit send. A few moments later, my phone dings. "She says she's thrilled for us and will call us later. Also, she and her husband are trying to get time off work to come to Harmony Lake for a visit."

"Thanks for the warning," Eric teases with a wink. "I'll enjoy the peace and quiet in the meantime."

"I know it's always exciting when my sister comes to town," I admit. "But it's not like anyone has ever died or anything."

Not yet.

KEEP READING for a sneak peek of Life Crafter Death: A Knitorious Murder Mystery book 9

LIFE CRAFTER DEATH

CHAPTER 1

Friday, October 1st

We live ten hours apart, but I see my sister, Emmy, almost every day. Millions of people see her every day. She co-hosts the popular morning show, *Hello, today!*

"Good girl, Soph," I say as the corgi brushes past my legs and through the open door.

She propels herself off the deck and onto the frost-covered lawn, triggering the motion detector which illuminates the pre-dawn backyard with harsh, artificial light.

While Sophie does her business and conducts her first perimeter check of the day, I fix her breakfast, drop a pumpkin spice coffee pod in the coffeemaker, and turn on the TV to catch my daily glimpse of my sister.

The TV comes to life, permeating the family room and kitchen with *Hello, today!*'s snappy theme music. I retrieve my mug from the coffeemaker and savour the first glorious sip of soul-satisfying caffeine while watching the title sequence. Cast and crew member names fade in and out as my sister zooms across the TV screen, riding a Segway through the studio. Then the camera cuts to footage of her and her co-host cooking with a celebrity chef. Then another cut to footage of Emmy drinking from an oversized *Hello, today!* mug while someone touches up her hair and makeup. She and the makeup artist burst into laughter.

Hello, today! is a typical infotainment morning show. Two co-hosts and their colleagues broadcast live, cycling between news, traffic, weather, and sports updates, interspersed with lifestyle and human interest segments.

It's early, and the world is still dark and quiet, but I'm wide awake. As a reluctant morning person, I'm wired to wake up early. I envy people whose internal clocks let them sleep past dawn, but I'm not one of them. This time of year, when the days are shorter, I'm up and at 'em before the sun.

Sophie scratches at the back door, and I look away from the TV to let her in. Sophie shakes off the early morning chill, buries her face in her food dish, and devours her breakfast with enthusiasm.

"...is filling in for Miranda Monroe, who's under the weather. Feel better, Miranda!"

I spin and look at the TV when Rich Kendall—

pronounced Rich Ken-doll—announces that my sister isn't at work today. Apparently, she's sick.

Miranda Monroe is my sister's given name and the name she uses professionally. Our names are almost identical, not our parents' most creative moment. They named me Megan Elizabeth Monroe, and named my sister, Miranda Elizabeth Monroe.

According to our father, when Emmy was born, sixteen-month-old me had yet to develop the necessary verbal skills to pronounce Miranda. My garbled attempt to say my baby sister's name sounded like Emmy, so that's what everyone called her. It stuck. Friends and family still call her Emmy. Despite three marriages, and three name changes, Emmy has always used her maiden name on television.

I whip my phone out of my housecoat pocket and check my text messages. Emmy always texts me when she misses work. Always. No text. I type a quick message.

Me: Are you OK? Rich said you're sick.

I hit send and stare at the screen, waiting for the three dots to appear that show my sister is typing a reply. We always reply to each other's texts right away. No dots. Hmmm.

"Good morning, Mrs. Sloane!" Eric says, shutting the front door behind him.

"Umm… we're not married yet," I remind him with a grin.

"I know. I'm practicing. I like the way it sounds."

Eric Sloane is my fiancé and chief of the Harmony Lake Police Department.

I scrunch my nose at his muskiness when he kisses me good morning.

His skin glistens and his short, dark hair is damp with sweat. He just finished a run. I can't imagine running this early—scratch that—I can't imagine running. Eric possesses a terrifying and impressive amount of self-discipline.

"Hug?" he teases, his open arms drawing attention to the sweat-soaked shirt clinging to his fat-free, well-muscled torso.

"After you have a shower," I reply, taking a step backward, just in case he's serious.

He squats to greet Sophie, who's tippy-tapping her paws on the floor at his feet, waiting for him to notice her.

"Where's Emmy?" Eric lifts his chin toward the TV, where Emmy's usual spot on the *Hello, today!* sofa is occupied by the person who provides weather updates.

"Rich said she's sick."

I check my phone again, in case my sister replied to my text, and I missed the notification.

"Is she OK?" Eric asks, squeezing his eyebrows together.

"I don't know," I reply, shaking my head. "She hasn't answered my text."

"I'm sure she's fine," Eric assures me, sensing my

concern. "It's probably just a cold or something. She probably went back to bed."

"Probably," I agree.

My phone dings.

"See," Eric says, "that's her. Telling you she's fine."

I nod in acknowledgement and unlock my phone. It's a text, but not from Emmy. It's from my best friend, April.

"April," I tell Eric with a sigh. "She's asking if Emmy is OK because she's not on *Hello, today*!"

"How's their trip?" Eric asks.

April and her wife are out of town for a family wedding. They won't be back until next Friday. This is the longest April and her wife have ever left their bakery. April's wife is a talented pastry chef and together they own Artsy Tartsy, Harmony Lake's local bakery. While they're away, their pastry-chef friend is working at the bakery, staying at their house, and taking care of their cats.

"They're having a great time," I reply to Eric's question. "It helps that Marla is working at the bakery every day and texting them regular, reassuring updates."

Marla is one of my part-time employees. While April and Tamara are away, she's splitting her part-time hours between my yarn store, Knitorious, and Artsy Tartsy.

"Do you need me to help at the store today?" Eric offers.

Eric isn't working today. He's using some time off the department owes him for overtime he's worked.

"No, thanks," I reply. "You should enjoy your day off, not spend it shelving yarn and cashing out customers."

"I enjoy hanging out at Knitorious." He winks. "I have a huge crush on the owner. I can't stay away from her." With a glint of playful mischief in his brown eyes, Eric cocks one eyebrow and takes a step toward me. "Can you go in late? We could have breakfast together or something."

A familiar twinge of temptation tugs at me from deep inside, but my overdeveloped sense of responsibility overrides my desire to play hooky.

"I can't," I say, wishing I could. "We're short-staffed with Marla helping at the bakery.

"There are plenty of odd jobs to keep me busy at home today," Eric says with a sigh. "But if you want to come home for lunch…" he winks.

"I'll do my best," I say. "And I'll give Sophie the day off to keep you company."

Sophie's ears perk up when she hears her name. She comes to work with me every day, but she'll be happy to stay home with Eric.

"I'm sure Emmy is fine," Connie insists, tucking her sleek silver bob behind her ear. "She's probably asleep, and she'll text you when she wakes up."

Connie is my other part-time employee. She was the original owner of Knitorious. I worked for her part time until she retired, then I took over the store. Connie and I are more than colleagues, we're family. Chosen family. Connie and I met when I moved to Harmony Lake almost twenty years ago. I was only twenty-one years old, new in town, lonely, and overwhelmed. My husband was an ambitious young lawyer who spent most of his time at his office in the city. My daughter, Hannah, was a baby and I was a new, anxious mother. To top it off, my own mother had recently passed away unexpectedly. I was overwhelmed. To cope, I channeled my energy into knitting while Hannah slept. One day, realizing I'd knitted through my yarn stash, I pushed Hannah's stroller into Knitorious and met Connie. She took us under her wing and filled the mother and grandmother-shaped holes in our hearts.

"I'd feel better if I knew for sure," I respond.

"Who's Emmy?" Tina asks from a sofa in the cozy sitting area, her eyes laser-focused on the stitch she's knitting.

Tina Duran is new to Harmony Lake. She moved here a few months ago, looking for a fresh start after her divorce. She works at one of the mountain resorts. Tina's also a novice knitter, and Connie has been guiding and encouraging her on her knitting journey.

"Emmy is my sister," I reply. "She hasn't returned my text, which is out of character for her."

I don't explain that Emmy is Miranda Monroe, the popular television morning show host.

Today, Tina's learning how to knit in the round by making Knitted Knockers. Every October, in honour of Breast Cancer Awareness Month, the Harmony Lake Charity Knitting Guild makes and donates Knitted Knockers. These are handmade breast prostheses for women who have undergone mastectomies or other breast procedures.

"I'm sure you'll hear from her," Tina says.

I'm about to agree with Tina when my phone dings.

"Maybe it's Emmy!" Connie suggests optimistically, reaching for my phone on the counter and handing it to me. "She probably went back to bed and just woke up."

I unlock my phone and look at the screen with a heavy sigh.

"It's April." I exhale and place the phone on the coffee table in front of me. "She sent me a funny video of a cat using dog treats to get a German Shepherd to do tricks." I smile at Connie. "If Emmy hasn't texted me by this afternoon, I'll phone her."

Tina places her knitting in her lap. "Maybe her phone died or something." She shrugs and places her knitting in her backpack, then slings her backpack over one shoulder, and stands up. "I have to go to work."

I suspect Tina is around my age, forty-one, or in her late thirties, but it's hard to tell, and it would be rude to ask. Her style of dress and the way she talks makes her seem younger, but Tina refers to movies, and music that I grew up with, which makes me think she looks younger than her actual age. Her dark hair shows no signs of grey, her brown eyes are bright, and her complexion is smooth and ageless. She has a hint of an accent that's difficult to place, but lovely to listen to. She says her accent is a combination of all the places she's lived. She was born in Brazil, but went to university in Europe. Then, after she got married, she moved around the US and Canada for her husband's job.

"I hope you hear from your sister," Tina says with a smile.

Connie and I wish her a good day, and she leaves.

"Mothballs!" Connie mutters her version of an expletive.

"What's wrong?"

"Tina left her jacket," Connie replies, pointing to the jacket draped over the back of the sofa. "That girl always leaves something behind," Connie muses, picking up the jacket and smoothing it over her arm. "I'll hang it up in the backroom."

"I'll send her a text so she knows where she left it," I offer.

According to my phone, it's almost lunchtime. I'll wait one more hour, then if I still haven't heard from Emmy, I'll phone her.

I try to focus on texting Tina, but I can't quiet the voice inside my head. It's a constant whisper warning me the reason I haven't heard from Emmy is because something is wrong. Very wrong.

Chapter 2

Connie is on her lunch break, and I'm washing the floor-to-ceiling display windows to distract myself from worrying about Emmy.

I flinch when the door swings open and slams against the wall with enough force to shake the yarn shelves and cause the bell to make a startling, loud crash.

"Emmy?" I blink and do a double take when my sister swoops into the store. "What are you doing here? Are you OK?" I ask, shocked to see her but relieved that she appears healthy and unharmed.

"It's over!" Emmy announces, throwing her hands into the air. "Phone Adam. I need him to represent me in the divorce!" she demands, sniffling. "Again," she adds under her breath.

Adam Martel is my ex-husband. He's also Harmony Lake's resident lawyer and our town's mayor. He represented Emmy in her first two divorces.

"What happened?" I ask, stepping out of the display window.

I close the door, making sure Emmy's dramatic entrance didn't damage it or the wall.

"Armando wants to destroy my career," she announces. "The network asked us to be contestants on the next season of *Perfect Match*. The big wigs think it will draw *Hello, today!* viewers to *Perfect Match*, and draw *Perfect Match* viewers to *Hello, today!*" She breaks into sobs. "Armando refused! Can you believe that, Sis? This is a huge career opportunity for me. Why does he hate me?" Emmy bursts into tears and sobs into a wadded-up tissue clenched in her fist.

I envelop my sister in a hug, and she collapses into my arms.

Armando Garcia is Emmy's husband. He's a professional soccer player. They've been married for three years, but I don't know Armando very well because his hectic schedule keeps him on the road most of the year. He's rarely available to accompany my sister when she visits Harmony Lake, and whenever I visit her, he's away playing soccer.

Perfect Match is a reality television show where eight B-list celebrity couples live in the *Perfect Match* house, sequestered from the outside world. Each week they face a challenge designed to test the strength of their relationship. A challenge could be something like one person being tempted by an attractive distraction, someone's former flame showing up, dealing with rumours about each other, or one person being encouraged by their housemates to keep a secret from their partner. Drama, strategic alliances, and secret relationships ensue. Each week, the home audience votes online to determine which couple failed the weekly challenge. Then, at the start of the next episode, the host reveals last week's disgraced couple and evicts them from the *Perfect Match* house. This continues until one couple remains; the last couple wins the title of *Perfect Match* and gets to return for the tournament of champions called *Perfect Match: Playing With Fire*. I don't watch the show. The concept doesn't appeal to me. Relationships are hard enough without competing to prove your love for each other in front of a prime-time audience. I understand why Armando would rather not take part.

"Did Armando say why?" I ask, leading Emmy to the cozy sitting area and helping her into an overstuffed chair.

"He says filming will interfere with soccer," Emmy snorts, rolling her eyes. "Also, *Brad*,"—Emmy sneers with contempt when she says his name—"told him appearing on the show would *devalue the Armando Garcia brand*. Whatever that means." She blows her nose. "Brad hates me!"

Brad Hendricks is Armando's agent. He negotiates Armando's sponsorship deals, media appearances, and such.

"I'm sure Brad doesn't hate you," I reassure her, having no actual insight into Brad's feelings about my sister.

"He's always hated me, and this is another way for him to sabotage my marriage." She breaks into a fresh fit of sobs. "Armando doesn't see it. He thinks Brad is his friend. If Armando had listened to me and found a new agent when we got married, I wouldn't be here right now."

"Maybe Armando doesn't want to spend the little time you have together filming a reality TV show," I suggest, trying to temper her extreme perspective while I hand her a box of tissues.

It's amazing how little time my sister and her husband spend together. Between training camp, preseason games, regular season games, postseason games, and public appearances, Armando travels over two hundred days each year. Emmy's Monday-to-Friday job on *Hello, today!* keeps her anchored to their hometown, and she devotes much of her time off to promotional appearances for worthy causes and for the network.

The bell above the door jingles—gentler this time—and Sophie appears at our feet, wagging her Corgi tail and panting. Torn between visiting me or Emmy first, Emmy wins and Sophie places her front paws on her knees.

"Hey, Soph," Emmy whispers, scratching Sophie between the ears.

"Emmy! This is a pleasant surprise," Eric says, then he looks at me. "See! I told you she was OK." He smiles at Emmy, and she looks up at him with her watery eyes and quivering chin. He looks at me again. "She's not OK, is she?"

I shake my head.

Eric places a to-go cup from Latte Da on the counter. A chocolate caramel latte, my current favourite specialty coffee from their fall menu. The chocolaty coffee aroma makes my mouth water from ten feet away.

"It's nice to see you, Eric," Emmy says, standing up and giving him a hug. "Megan, I'll be right back. I need to freshen up."

"Of course," I say, rubbing her back reassuringly. "Take your time."

Emmy tosses her bag over her shoulder and heads toward the backroom with Sophie guiding the way.

"What's going on?" Eric whispers.

"Domestic quarrel," I whisper in reply.

He nods and his mouth forms a tiny **o**.

"I told Adam I'd meet him for a round of golf later," Eric explains. "But I'll cancel if you need me."

Yes, my fiancé and my ex-husband are friends. Good friends. They golf and watch sports together. It was weird at first, but we're all used to it now. Adam and I might be divorced, but we're still family and have forged a strong friendship from the wreckage of our marriage. We're determined to keep our family intact for the sake of our daughter, and Eric supports that.

"Thank you, honey, but go. This could be your last round of the year," I say, referring to the unseasonable, summer-like weather we've enjoyed this week.

"Are you sure?" Eric looks unconvinced.

"Positive." I stand on my tippy toes and give him a

kiss. Eric is almost a foot taller than me, so even when I wear heels, kissing requires some stretching on my part and some stooping on his. "Connie will be back from lunch soon, and Emmy's exhausted, so I'll probably send her home to rest. If you're golfing, the house will be quiet for her."

Persuaded to keep his golf date, Eric kisses my fore-head, reminds me to call him if I need anything, and leaves. On his way out, he holds the door open for Tina as she rushes into Knitorious, breathless and flushed as if she ran here.

"Hey, Tina," I greet her with a smile. "You seem like you're in a hurry."

"Kind of." Tina nods and catches her breath. "I'm on my break and came to pick up my jacket."

"Right," I say, remembering Connie saying some-thing about hanging Tina's jacket in the backroom. "Connie put it in the back. I'll get for you."

Tina's jacket isn't hanging on the coat rack by the back door, and at first glance, it's not in the closet. I turn on the closet light and slide the hangers over one by one.

"Aha! Found you!" I inform the jacket with a smug sense of victory when I find it squashed between two parkas that belong to the tenants who live in the apart-ment above the store.

"Got it," I announce, striding from the backroom to the front of the store.

Tina can't hear me because she's mesmerized by Emmy's presence. I guess Tina watches *Hello, today!* and knows who Miranda Monroe is. Emmy must've slipped past me and returned to the store while I was in the closet, searching for Tina's jacket. Tina is captivated by Emmy. Her eyes are wide, and her mouth is ajar, yet smiling.

"You're even prettier in person," Tina gushes with an awestruck expression plastered to her face.

"Thank you," Emmy smiles graciously. "You're gorgeous, by the way. Your complexion is spectacular. Tell me about your skin care regimen."

Being the true professional she is, you'd never guess Emmy is in emotional distress and just spent ten hours travelling. Her superpower is turning off Emmy Garcia and turning on Miranda Monroe with less effort than it takes to flip a light switch.

"Soap and water," Tina giggles with a shrug. "And lots of moisturizer. Especially in the cold months when the air is dry."

"It's all about the moisturizer," my sister agrees.

"Why are you in Harmony Lake?" Tina asks Emmy as I approach them at the counter. "Are you here to buy yarn? Are you a knitter?"

"Our mother taught us both how to knit," Emmy explains, jerking her head toward me. "I go through knitting phases every few years, but I'm not as dedicated as Megan."

"Miranda Monroe is your sister?" Tina asks, staring

at me, dumbfounded. "The same sister you worried about this morning?"

"This is her," I confirm, smiling.

"But I thought your sister's name is Emmy?" Tina scrunches her brows together in confusion.

"Emmy is my nickname," my sister explains. "My given name is Miranda, but friends and family call me Emmy. You can call me Emmy." She flashes Tina a thousand-watt smile.

"I can?" Tina asks, mesmerized. "I'm glad you're OK, Emmy. Megan was worried."

Emmy looks at me and puts her hand on mine. "I'm sorry I didn't let you know I was coming ahead of time. It was an impromptu decision." She sighs. "I was incommunicado during the flight. I saw your texts when I landed and meant to reply from the rental car, but I couldn't get my phone to connect to the car, and it's not safe to text and drive. I told myself I'd text you when I pulled over, but I drove straight through. I didn't mean to worry you."

"You're here now," I say.

"Now that I know you're sisters, I can see the resemblance," Tina observes.

Either Tina's skills of observation are superhuman, or the resemblance she claims to see is wishful thinking. There is no resemblance and hasn't been for at least a decade. We used to have the same curly brown hair, but Emmy dyes her hair blonde now. Her colourist does an amazing job. Unless you knew her before her blonde phase, you'd never guess Emmy isn't a natural blonde. And regular Brazilian blowouts keep her curls at bay and ensure her hair is smooth, shiny, and bouncy. Growing up, we had the same fair skin, but regular appointments with a spray tanner give Emmy's complexion a year-round, sun-kissed shimmer. We both inherited our father's hazel eyes, but thanks to the miracle of tinted contact lenses, Emmy's eyes are closer to emerald green than hazel. Our body shapes have always been different. My curvy, hourglass figure is courtesy of our mother, while Emmy inherited her narrow, petite frame and delicate features from our father's side of the family. I've always been jealous of Emmy's ability to wear spaghetti straps without a bra, and I always will be.

The only physical traits Emmy and I still have in common are our height and shoe size. I suspect my sister has had some Botox because her face is suspiciously smooth for forty. She's only sixteen months younger than me, and I'm sure my forehead lines and crow's feet were well-established sixteen months ago. Compared to my sister's mannequin-like skin, my skin looks like it was made by Rand McNally.

"I wish I could stay and hang out with you all afternoon," Tina announces, throwing her jacket over her arm. "But my break is only an hour. If I don't leave now, I'll be late getting back to work."

"I'm sure we'll see each other again," Emmy assures her. "I'll be in town for a few days."

Tina leaves, and with the flip of an invisible switch, television personality Miranda Monroe disappears and my sister, Emmy Garcia takes her place.

"Emmy?" Connie drops her purse on the counter. "What a wonderful surprise." She walks toward Emmy with her arms wide. "We worried when you weren't on *Hello, today!* this morning.

"Hi, Connie." Emmy stands up, and I can tell she's fending off a fresh round of tears.

"Oh, my," Connie says when my sister, sobbing, falls into her arms, leaving an emotional puddle on the hardwood floor. "There, there, Emmy. Shhhh." Connie's blue eyes fill with the moisture of sympathetic tears.

As they sway, Connie smoothes Emmy's hair and murmurs reassuring things.

Connie is in her element. She's the most motherly woman I know, and it's never more obvious than when she unleashes her maternal instincts to comfort someone.

After they pull apart, Emmy explains to Connie that her marriage is over, and she came to Harmony Lake to process everything in a supportive, private environment. Then, worried that another fan might show up and she'll have to flip the magic switch that summons Miranda Monroe, my sister excuses herself again to freshen up.

"Why don't you take Emmy home, my dear," Connie suggests. "She's exhausted. Get her settled in your guest room, and I'll take care of the store."

"Are you sure?" I ask. "I hate to leave you on your own."

"It's not busy today. I'll be fine," Connie insists. "Emmy is distraught. She travelled ten hours for love and support."

"You're right," I admit, feeling guilty for worrying about work when my sister feels like her life is falling apart. "I'll take Emmy home."

Read the rest of Life Crafter Death today!

ALSO BY REAGAN DAVIS

Knit One Murder Two

Killer Cables

Murder & Merino

Twisted Stitches

Son of a Stitch

Crime Skein

Rest In Fleece

Life Crafter Death

Neigbourhood Swatch: A Knitorious Cozy Mystery Short Story

Sign up for Reagan Davis' email list to be notified of new releases and special offers: www.ReaganDavis.com Follow Reagan Davis on Amazon

Follow Reagan Davis on Facebook and Instagram

ABOUT THE AUTHOR

Reagan Davis doesn't really exist. She is a pen name for the real author who lives in the suburbs of Toronto with her husband, two kids, and a menagerie of pets. When she's not planning the perfect murder, she enjoys knitting, reading, eating too much chocolate, and drinking too much Diet Coke. The author is an established knitwear designer who regularly publishes individual patterns and is a contributor to many knitting books and magazines. I'd tell you her real name, but then I'd have to kill you. (Just kidding! Sort of.)

http://www.ReaganDavis.com/

25190290R00182